Also by Elle M Drew

<u>The Shifters of Garoureve</u>

One Night in Garoureve

Needed in Garoureve

Trapped in Garoureve

Return to Garoureve

Book 5 (2026)

Book 6 (2026)

<u>The Shifters of Bear Valley</u>

Owen

Cedric

Gareth (Fall 2026)

<u>Monstrous Novellas</u>

The Vampire in the Bookstore

Tempted by Tentacles

The Werewolf in the Brewery (Summer 2026)

<u>Mafia Omegaverse</u>

Devoted Destruction

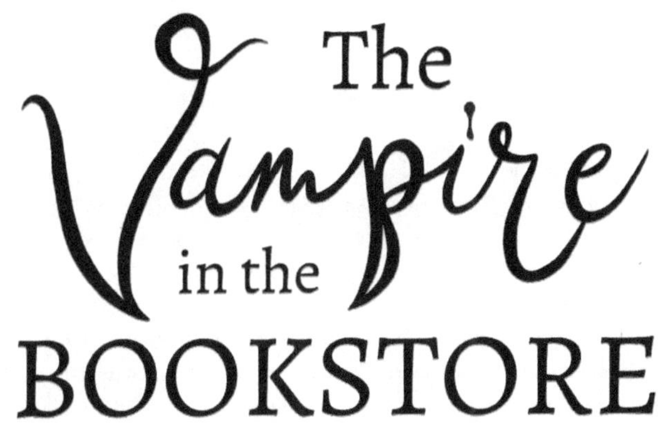

ELLE M DREW

Cover Design by Rowan Merrick, www.rowanmerrick.com

Edited by R.N. Barbosa, www.barbosbooks.com

Author's Note

Dear reader, please note The Vampire in the Bookstore contains the following...

Sexual Content, including the following kinks: Biting, Pain, Blood, Choking, Primal Play, and Praise.

There is also stalking, morally gray main characters, and technically an age gap, as he is an ancient vampire and she is in her thirties.

There is, throughout, the description of feeling high from blood, along with the death of a side character on page.

There is also the rebirth of a main character on page.

And, as you can likely guess by the title... there is bibliophilia.

Please take care of yourself before reading!

xoxo Elle

in which a vampire enters a bookstore

In all his centuries, Declan had never tired of the scent of his two most favorite things. The first, of course, was blood. The life force of humans teeming in the air, knowing that it would soon be on his tongue, restoring him, rushing through his otherwise dried veins. The scent of it drew his vampiric nature to the surface with a single whiff, making every hair on his body stand up, and sharpening his focus until he was satiated.

The second, however, was not one tied at all to his vampiric nature. It was instead tied to who he was as a man, or at least, whatever was left of the man he had been so many eons ago. Books. He would never tire of the scent of books.

They were a blend of many things, and had changed over the centuries, and yet, his love of them never once faded. Once it had been the scent of skins pulled taut and dried, and of the parchment within, marked with ink written with quills and lit by candles as he worked. Now it was the scent of printed ink on paper, with bindings and glue. It was all a fragrance which called to him.

Whether the scent was of an old book, long preserved within a collection, one he was about to add to his own, or one freshly written, the author a child compared to his many years, it did not matter. The scent of books would always draw him within.

Particularly when the scent of humans was *not* within.

That was not to say he did not enjoy the scent of humans. They carried blood within their veins what served as a life force to him and his kind. And yet, being around them, around their questions... They were in such a hurry. No large wonder, given how short their lives were, but they were like little ants, climbing and rushing about. They had such carelessness in their manner, with no appreciation for that which was old, and that which would soon be lost.

But also, when around humans, he always gave into his baser desires. The desire for blood, for flesh, for sex—it was overwhelming to be surrounded by so many.

It was why he enjoyed his large manor in the quiet countryside, and why he enjoyed smaller towns, where he could simply walk and enter and then step out and disappear as needed.

The problem was, most small towns ceased to exist, save in small patches once it was dark, including the bookshop.

And, as a vampire who hoarded books like dragons hoarded their wealth... it was a major inconvenience.

With the changing of seasons, night arrived earlier. A fortunate thing, but still not early enough for him to peruse the shelves as he often preferred, but instead forcing him to... *rush*. He couldn't savor the soft fragrance of the books, the feeling of worn leather binding in his hands, nor could he take his time to decide. Should he leave a book on the shelf, there was always the chance a collector would call during the day to snatch it out of his grasp.

What if, in his rush, he missed a true prize?

Ah, but it was out of his control. All he could do, as he approached the bookshop, was not waste his time. It was one of the few in the area which regularly accepted books from large estate sales, so there was no telling what delights were hidden among the shelves. And, if he was fortunate, it would not be the old woman behind the counter, but her much younger assistant. The younger one always agreed to stay open a few minutes later, knowing he would only stay if he planned to make another large purchase.

His vampiric nature helped as well, given how she responded to his aura.

Humans were always funny little things when facing a vampire. Some became belligerent and paranoid, while others became giving and docile. It was a flip of the coin, one which Declan would always risk in pursuit of a book.

He was disappointed, however, to see the old woman stacking books in the corner when he entered. If it were not for her love of books, and estate sales, he would have disposed of her long ago, but he feared that once she went, so too would the shop. No, despite her being a regular pain, she had to be protected, for the sake of the books. He would simply have to return again in a few nights and waste no time with the precious half hour he had left before the shop closed.

Giving a nod to the old woman, Declan walked along the rows of shelves. Most books were typically organized by genre or focus, but new arrivals were kept separate, waiting not just to be sorted, but so collectors such as himself could easily focus on things they had not yet seen. It was an area often ignored, given that the resale of books did not seem too popular anymore, with so many using the electronic devices to read. It meant he was often alone, which suited him fine. He preferred the companionship of books above all others.

A good trait for a vampire.

What could be better company for an immortal than the written word of the past? They were relics of a long-forgotten time, some from even before his own days of walking the earth. There could never be too many books, for with each passing year, more and more discoveries were made. He had even, after some concern, discovered the wonders of an electronic reader. Manuscripts which he would be quite unable to get his hands on, could at least exist in a form in his library, until such a point in time as he could have a replica made.

He liked that he could easily read any text on a handheld device, but the feeling of a book in his hands was better than the feeling of anything else.

And the scent of books, mixed with the scent of blood, and a soft woman underneath him, giving it to him freely, and—

Declan froze where he stood, just inside the small alcove where new arrivals sat on waiting shelves. A woman stood in front of them, her back to him. The scent of books flowed from her like ambrosia, drawing and urging him in without even thinking. The last time he had faced such a reaction, he had been lured in by a vampire.

But this woman was no vampire. He could hear the whispers of blood moving through her veins, and could already feel the warmth radiating from her. Given her lack of reaction to his presence, it was also apparent that she was not a supernatural of any sort. There was no stiffening to her shoulders, no glance, no turning about. She was completely at ease, lost in the book currently in her grasp, with her neck exposed to an apex predator.

A neck that was... for want of a better description... ripe and supple. The freckles on her skin seemed perfectly poised for him to sink his teeth into, like targets for him so he did not otherwise mar her skin. And yet, he so wished to see his mark upon her, with her blood dripping a trail for his tongue to follow. Would she taste like the books whose scent rolled off her? What could she possibly do that would have the blend of leather and grass, and vanilla and tobacco all clinging to her like a second skin?

He had to know... And he had to see if the freckles trailing across her throat were also on the inside of her thighs.

Thighs which, unfortunately, were covered in fabric. In fact, most of her was well covered. From head to toe, all he could see was her neck and her hands, although they too were nearly engulfed by her sweater.

And her face. He could not see it yet, as she was studying the book in her grasp so intently, with pieces of hair obscuring what limited view the angle could afford him. But soon he would be able to see her face, if she would only glance in his direction.

He thought about clearing his throat, coughing slightly, or performing some other soft noise, to draw her attention to him, but he was still soaking in the warmth of a woman so near, so unaware of his presence. She was thoroughly wrapped up in whatever book she held, and he found that, for the first time in a very long time, he was more interested in the person holding the book than the book itself.

A true testament to the power of his nostrils, given how her scent alone had him mesmerized.

Ah, but it was also more than that. Everything about her was so unassuming, so... *plain*. Not that she was plain in any matter of sense, but nothing about her was meant to attract any attention. Nothing was flashy or loud. Her clothes were simple, of neutral colors, and her hair worn in a practical fashion, although a few pieces escaped the elastic, threatening to impede her vision.

She looked like a model, ready to be painted by one of the greatest of the Renaissance, or perhaps even into the early years of Baroque. She was relaxed, calm, and slow in a world that moved far too fast for a man of his age. There was a gentleness as her fingers moved down the page almost reverently, and he wondered what it would feel like to have that touch run down his chest, or across his fanged teeth.

She was so wholly focused on the book before her. It was as though looking in a mirror. A much more attractive mirror, of course, but...

He longed to know her. To know her name. To know her inside and out.

But how would one make such an introduction? He had not concerned himself with pleasantries in... generations, at the very least. Where once he had been courteous, using general airs and manners to attain that which was important to him, he had become a recluse in the last century. Humans were, for lack of better uses, only there for food or books. And this woman, while appetizing and holding a book...

She was more than that. And as such, she should be handled with care and grace. With more than just...

And now, he was failing for words. Who was he, that he was becoming so unlike himself over a human?

"Oh, I'm so sorry."

Declan's gaze pulled from where it had drifted on the bookshelf to the woman before him, now turning to face him. She had the voice of an angel... a sultry angel... but that was not what had captivated him. No, his attention was far more focused on her eyes. Deep and soulful, the darkest brown, they were the sort of eyes a man could get lost in.

If this woman were any sort of creature beyond human, he would be doomed. Even still...

"I can move out of your way if you're wanting to look at the books."

"You could never be in the way," Declan answered coolly, amazed at how steady his voice was, and how easily the words came to him. Years of practice, of evading those who might seek him out, had made him a far better orator than he had been in his human life. That was all that saved him now. "But I must ask, what is it about this book that has you so mesmerized?"

She looked away from him, pouting slightly as she inspected the book in her hands. He had to force his own gaze to follow hers, to look at the worn cover. There was nothing about it on the outside which looked to be remarkable, no ornate markings or hint as to what was within, but upon closer inspection, thanks to a step forward he had not intended to take, and his vampiric eyesight, he noted what a treasure she held.

"It's the stitching of the binding," the angel said as she carefully opened the book once more and showed him where two signatures met along the seam. "Hand-stitched. You rarely see it on the shelves, even in second-hand bookstores, and not with a simple vellum cover with no markings. I guess because this is a book on housekeeping from... over two hundred years ago... that no one considered it of any worth, but—"

"But you recognized it immediately," Declan pointed out in wonder. Who was this woman, that she could see value in something that others overlooked? "Do you work with older books often?"

"I do," she answered with a half-smile.

He waited for her to continue, to add something more on, to explain herself, but that half smile remained on her lips, teasing him, forcing him to ask if he wanted to get to know her more.

It was working. Whatever she was doing to him, whatever spell she was weaving over him, it was working.

He was entrapped, lured in by her expressive eyes, sultry lips, and enchanting bookish aura, and he was willing to walk directly into it, if only to learn a little more.

Others would call him a fool. A sentimental fool, to be lured in by a human.

But if death or danger came to him at her fingertips... he would go willingly.

"I'm Declan," he said, offering his hand. "And, I would like to hear more about your work with older books."

She stared at his offered hand, then carefully closed the book, tucking it against her chest while stepping forward. He noted the way her buttoned blouse lifted slightly, almost revealing... something... but his gaze then moved to her throat, hidden by the white collar of her shirt. He watched her swallow, the vein popping ever so slightly, reminding him that she was human, and the blood in her veins...

Would it taste like ink and parchment, and leather? Or would—

He could never know, because this woman could never be reduced to something as simple as sustenance. Her spirit, her very essence... her conversation and smile alone could sustain him another thousand years at the very least.

"Rosamund," she answered as her hand slipped into his, warming him immediately. "And I'd love to tell you all about it."

in which our heroine knows a secret

What the hell was she doing, and why was this working out better than she ever intended?

He was here. He was right in front of her. And she was talking to him. She had known that he frequented this shop on occasion, and she knew that a new delivery of books had come in, but to have this plan work out so perfectly…

In only a few aspects of her life was Rosamund a planner, and those were all academic. She always had a process for new acquisitions, and with restorations and preservations. She was excellent at planning and prepping meals. She thrived at things like planning her outfits so that she would be comfortable and professional, and not inhibited in any way from her work. She could plan!

But when it came to things like men? And when this particular man was a passion project…

It had entirely started all by accident, but she was always analytic and thorough in her research, and once the pieces were there, linking him together, it was easy to see that he had used two different names. The subject matter varied so significantly, but the styles were the same. When she had tracked him down, scoured for more information… well, she was a researcher. She had a theory, she researched it, and always found her answer.

Were some of her methods a bit questionable? Perhaps. Was she maybe a little bit creepy for her behavior? Probably.

But given how he was smiling at her and asking her about her research, and he *had* been the one to approach her in the store... Granted, she *knew* this would be the section he would journey to within the store, but...

Here he was. Declan Triarius. Not that she should technically know his last name, and she wasn't certain it was his real name, but it was the name he had placed on her *favorite* of his, and given the name he had offered...

She needed to pretend she knew nothing about the beautiful man in front of her. Because if he figured out that she had tracked him down on purpose, the embarrassment alone would kill her.

She should have let it go when she originally started chasing this man down, but once she knew something was connected, and once she had a lead, she had to meet him, just once. Even with knowing that a person should never meet their hero, not that he was a hero, but it was an old saying for a reason! She should know better than to track down someone who had had such an impact on her. And yet, she had to meet him on the off chance that he would have any interest in speaking to her.

And now, here she was, smiling at him like he was an old book or artifact, and he was smiling back, taking her hand, and introducing himself.

She should have had a plan. Something. Anything beyond teasing about work with old books. Because now, she was going to have to say something, and she didn't know what to say. At all.

It was hard to think when a man so effortlessly charming was smiling at her.

"Now, tell me more about your working with older books. It is rare indeed to find someone who shares a passion for older and worn things. For you to have noted the age and the binding so easily tells me that this... well, no. I would not want to assume anything, but I would hazard a guess that this is something more than a hobby for you."

"As you said, a passion," Rosamund agreed as she looked up from where their hands were still touching. He hadn't let go, and now, his thumb was brushing the back of her knuckles. It sent a shiver down her spine, and her already rapidly beating heart picked up speed. "But if you mean if I work with them professionally, then yes. I'm an archivist, specializing in older books, particularly the preservation of manuscripts that are falling apart. I always note the stitches along the binding."

His thumb continued the tender strokes a few moments longer before his hand tensed, and then he withdrew. She looked up, startled to see that he was now even taking a step back, and shaking his head slightly. Why was he pulling away? Had she said something wrong? Was it—No! This was an older bookshop. Anyone who had a love for older books would be within. Her work hadn't given her away, had it?

Had she already slipped up, so soon?

"My apologies," he rushed to explain, shaking himself slightly. "I did not mean to—"

He was looking at his hand, and she looked down at her own, realizing what his apology was for. He had been holding her hand, caressing it really, and that was...

Why was her heart still racing in her chest, and her blood still rushing through her veins?

"Oh, it's fine, promise. I'm—"

Rosamund didn't know what else to say. She had, once again, no plan at all. She should say something, right? Accept his apology, then find some way to bring the discussion back to books, or her studies, or him? He had been teasing at his own passion for books, and that was quite a way to describe it, but how could she redirect now that he was withdrawing?

"Would you like to look at the books?" she offered, taking a step to the side, no longer blocking the shelf which she was certain had been his original destination. "I was blocking your path, so—"

"As I said before, Rosamund, you could never be in the way. While I did originally plan to look for a book or two, I find that I have instead been led to you. And I find you to be far more interesting than any book this store contains."

A shiver ran down her spine and she smiled again, this one not coy and teasing, but instead filled with teeth, and maybe the tip of her tongue. Her, more interesting than books? She was an interesting person, to be certain, but nothing could be more interesting than books... save, perhaps, for him.

"You're teasing me. Nothing and no one could ever be more interesting than books." She clung to the one in her arms closer to her chest and rolled her eyes before glancing at the shelf. "The shop will be closing soon, so if you're searching for a book in particular, you should probably make that your priority, and not worry about talking to me."

Why was she... why was she teasing him into looking at *books* rather than at her? She needed a plan! Because directing him *away* from her was entirely contrary to *everything* she wanted at this moment.

She wanted his attention on her, wholly, fully. Not on the books, even if they were a shared passion of theirs.

Rosamund looked back to Declan, expecting to see him moving towards the shelf, but instead, he was looking at her. No, not looking.

He was analyzing her with his gaze. What was it she had said, or more likely done? What was making him study her like this?

"What? What is it?" she asked, her lips curling into a nervous smile. "Why are you looking at me like that?"

"A beautiful woman with a love for old books which rivals my own? Why wouldn't I be looking at you?"

Never in her life would Rosamund ever consider herself to be the sort of woman to be weak in her knees. She had very strong knees, thank you very much. Knees which were used to climbing ladders and kneeling to pull boxes from the back of a shelf.

And she was not a woman who would melt under the gaze of a man who had given her any sort of compliment. At all. She knew her worth, knew her measure.

And yet, this was not a man at all. In her eyes, he was practically a God. And here he was, complimenting her.

Her heart pounded in her chest, the steady beat a reminder to keep on task and figure out a plan, fast, before she screwed this up.

"You also like older books?" she fumbled, only to then shake her head slightly as she glanced away. She already knew the answer to that, of course, and not just because she knew who he was— "I'm sorry, obviously you do, to be back in this dusty corner with me. I doubt anyone who *doesn't* love old books would even know to look back here."

"It appears, Rosamund, that while both of us love the words written within these books, neither of us is very good at using any of them." He was the one teasing her now, a smile curling over his lips, revealing his teeth. She shivered as she forced herself to look into his dark eyes, away from the pearly whites.

"And who said I read the books?" she retorted, showing off her own teeth as she smiled. "I'm an archivist, not a librarian. Collecting books is a very different passion from actually reading them."

"Ahh, too true," he agreed, approaching her. He withdrew his hand from his pocket, and she almost expected him to reach toward her, but he paused beside the shelf and ran his forefinger along a leather spine.

She shivered, wanting to know that touch across her skin. It had been cold when they shook hands, but she knew his icy touch would burn her alive.

His fingers stopped, and she watched as he moved towards another book, running his thumb along the joint, and then to another. They were all different subjects, different wrappings, different eras. None of them had a pattern, as far as she could tell. His gaze was on the shelf, allowing her a moment to take in his profile.

He was shorter in stature than she had expected, not that she had expected a large man, and who was she to call anyone short when she was barely over five feet tall. If she was standing directly in front of him, his chin would be at her forehead, no more. Something about him had seemed larger than life in her head, bigger, grander. Instead, he was dressed simply, in worn, heavy-duty pants and a long-sleeved, collarless pullover, with the sleeves pushed up.

Nothing about this man screamed of how important he was, of how much prestige he had, and the wealth of knowledge within him.

She liked that. Liked that he was unassuming in his presence.

His fingers left the shelf as he turned towards her, his gaze taking her in slowly. The tip of his tongue flicked out over his lips but tucked itself away quickly. It felt like a tease, making her wonder why he had done such a thing. His eyes eventually met hers and she waited, breath held tight in her chest, for him to say or do something more.

"Why don't we start again?" he offered, taking two steps towards her to close the distance. He offered his hand once more, only this time, his palm was up and his fingers curled. It was not a handshake that he was offering her.

She reached out, sliding her fingers over his, and watched as he lifted her hand to his mouth, pressing a soft kiss to the back of it. A shuddered breath escaped her, an embarrassing thing really, her body responding to his touch in a way she hadn't ever imagined. There was a curl to his lips as he pulled away and looked up at her, her hand still held within his own.

"I'm Declan, and I have a love for older books and manuscripts. I enjoy finding old and worn treasures which haven't been touched in years, and restoring them to life. And I happen to enjoy reading the pages within, although I will admit I have not read every book within my collection, because as you mentioned, collecting books and reading books are two separate hobbies. While I will admit that I first entered this shop in search of treasures from a recent estate sale, I find the company in front of me much more interesting than anything on these shelves."

Oh... *oh*. Had she said she needed a plan? Because apparently, having no plan was currently working out quite well for her. Exceedingly well, particularly because if she had assembled any sort of an array of plans in her head, none would have outlined any sort of response to what was currently happening.

Because here he was, Declan Triarius, kissing the back of her hand and choosing her company over that of books.

As it turned out, his cold touch did indeed set her on fire.

"And you are?"

Rosamund smiled up at him as she forced herself to look away from their hands to gaze into his eyes. They were warmer than she had thought before, more golden than brown. She relaxed as she looked up at him, trying to find the words, but not in any rush to form them into a sentence. Nothing about him screamed that he was impatient for an answer, and his calm presence, the lack of urgency in his mannerisms, helped to ease the last of her nerves.

She wanted his attention, and now she had it. Apparently, all she had to do was be herself. Which would be easy, given that she had never pretended to be anything else.

"I'm Rosamund, and the pursuit of history and knowledge has always been a passion of mine. In turn, it became a love of preserving older artifacts and repairing them when necessary. My specialty is working with books, so I have quite the collection, although I think it would take an eternity to read all of them... And I—"

"And I'm ready to go home," cut in a grumpy voice.

Rosamund jerked away from Declan's hold as she looked towards the old woman. If the bookkeeper had been gruff earlier, she was downright mean now. Although, a glance at the large wall clock told her that the shop had closed a few minutes earlier. How had time passed so quickly? She hadn't been there for that long. It had been close to closing when Declan entered, but—

"Of course," Rosamund agreed and lifted the book in her hands. "May I still purchase a few books, or—"

"Add it to my account, please," Declan interjected, his focus now locked on the older woman. He looked so tense, his eyes dark, but he was smiling. It looked... fake. "So that we might leave your store sooner, allowing you to close up."

The pair looked to be locked in a staring contest. The older woman gave in after a few seconds with a wave of her hand. She bustled over to look at the book in Rosamund's grasp, then nodded before giving them another brush of her hands, shooing them out.

Rosamund picked up her bag from a bookshelf and tucked her new treasure within. She was stalling for time, to find a way to continue their conversation, or their reintroduction, now that they were being pushed out onto the street. Declan held the door for her as they approached, and she gave him a nod and a smile as she stepped into the chilly fall evening. Despite her sweater, she shivered slightly but forced herself to ignore it.

Something, a plan. She needed a plan again to keep his attention, and to continue their conversation.

If they separated now there was no guarantee she would be able to find him again. It had taken her months to track him down to this shop, and it had been by chance that they encountered one another this evening.

"Well, it appears as though—"

"Dinner. Would you like to be dinner? *Have* dinner, I mean. With me."

He was flustered, and a smile curled back over her lips once more. Right. There was no need for a plan, because without her even trying his attention was once more fully on her.

"I would love dinner. And to continue this conversation."

"There's a smaller restaurant nearby where we could—"

"Lead the way!"

Attention caught, gained, and now, continuing.

All according to, well, plan. Or lack thereof.

Amazing.

in which our vampire finds himself hungry

By all the Gods, if he sunk his teeth into her supple skin, it would... he would...

Fuck. This was the problem with humans. They were so fragile, their life a flimsy thing which could be snapped away from them in an instant. And this human in particular, Rosamund. Beautiful, ethereal. She practically glowed in front of him, particularly when speaking about a book, or even just looking at him. He needed to know if the ink and parchment had seeped into her blood, her love of books something he could taste.

If there was ever such a thing as a perfect human to trap him, it was a creature such as this. Lucious and soft, with full lips and expressive eyes, and a passion that rivaled his own. It made him tongue-tied, even slipping so far as to ask if he could have her for dinner.

No, not dinner. Dessert. She would be the perfect dessert after his meal, for he would have to sink his teeth into another human before laying his hands on her once more, lest he accidentally kill her when he broke skin and tasted her very essence. No, he would savor every moment of her time, every word she uttered, and then once she was soft and pliant under him, he would taste her, taste her skin in all ways, both as a vampire and as a man.

Only if she was willing, of course, but he could smell it on her, could even taste it in the air. She was attracted to him, as much as he was attracted to her. She wanted his attention, bloomed under it, and he...

What were they keeping in the bowels of her university, that she had emerged with such potency that he was so thoroughly ensnared by her very aura?

So on edge was he, that when the old woman had interrupted them, interrupted *her*, Declan had been ready to rip the woman's throat out, bookstore and future manuscripts be damned. He had her opening up to him, a true and pure rose that needed careful protection to blossom under. She was nervous, although not about him, and the way she was responding to *his* aura was curious. She was curious. And he had to know more.

He had to know the taste of her blood on his tongue as she squirmed under him, clenching around his fingers, riding the high of both the venom in his fangs and the pleasure of his touch. He wanted to break her, to mold her. Wanted to feel her flutter around him. Wanted to soak in her very life, her strength, her ability. He wanted her knowledge, her passion, her drive. Wanted her—

"Thank you for the book. You didn't have to pay, you know. I could have paid for myself."

Declan shivered as the warmth of her voice washed over his cold body, pretending it was the wind. His willpower was strong, thanks to centuries of fighting the urge to sink his teeth into every living creature around him. Even so, it was being tested around her. He would have to watch himself, and be careful, or else he would push too far, too fast.

Dinner was an excellent idea, as it would allow them time to talk, and for her to relax around him, to become used to his presence. He wanted to know her real thoughts about him, without his influence overpowering her mind. She would have to grow used to his aura. And dinner was an excellent way for him to feed. Someone within the establishment would make a fine meal.

And food. He did like food on occasion.

It was very human to invite a woman for a meal. Very natural. She would suspect nothing, of course. He would ask about her work, about her current projects, her preferred era of study, if she studied history or information science before becoming an archivist, why she preferred archival work over discovery, and then...

Then, he would invite her to his home, to peruse his own library, and enjoy a dessert. The dessert being her, of course.

He could practically taste her already...

"Declan?"

"Apologies, sweet Rosamund." Declan stopped in his steps to turn towards her, taking her in with his vampire senses rather than the human ones.

She was breathing slowly, as though trying to purposely keep it steady and low, and her cheeks were red, likely from the cold wind, but possibly from his compliment. Ah, no, it was spreading across the tip of her nose now. That was a blush. For him. She was smiling as well, her plump lips enticing him to bite them, but he resisted. Needed to resist. Desperately.

"The wind, it is loud," he explained as he offered her his arm.

Why had he not done so when they left the bookstore? He had no explanation, but he was a gentleman. Or at least, had pretended to be for a variety of centuries. He should act like one.

"And I would prefer to give you my full attention once we are inside. The book is a small thing, a token of my appreciation for a conversation that I know will be enlightening, and for the pleasure of your company. You are giving me the gift of your time, which is a fleeting thing, I imagine, so I am grateful for it."

Rosamund smiled up at him again, somehow brighter than before. She took his arm, her small hand tucked against his forearm. He had not bothered to push down his sleeves, to cover up his bare skin, and he was glad of it. Glad that he could feel the softness of her touch on his own skin. She was softer than silk, softer than lace, and he knew it was likely oil from working with leather covers. How *divine*.

"Time is only fleeting if you feel as though you have been wasting it," she answered softly. "And I highly doubt an evening with you could ever be considered such."

Oh, such a sweet creature... if only she knew.

Declan resumed their walk, reaching the small restaurant in a few brief minutes. Never had he entered the place, but the aroma wafting onto the streets was always appealing, beyond the patrons themselves. He was not one for eating human food with any regularity, having no requirement for such sustenance in eons, but he enjoyed the occasional delicacy in his travels. Eating for pleasure and to enjoy something new, or recall a memory that could only be brought to him via taste.

But his own palate was not the one he worried about pleasing this evening. He knew nothing of her desires, of her own tastes, of her perhaps allergies or dislikes. She had raised no complaint about the restaurant, so perhaps she had dined there before? Or, perhaps she was simply amenable to anything, given his presence. Well, he would have to be certain she was pleased. He wanted to feed her, to satisfy her, to delight her.

He was centuries old with all the wealth in the world at his disposal, should he reach for it, and the ability to give her anything she desired.

Declan regretted his decision to bring her to the restaurant the moment they stepped within. It was too loud, not intimate enough.

What if she wasn't interested in anything on their menu? What if she had allergies or things she didn't like? Was this even a place she would enjoy?

"Mmm, something smells delicious," Rosamund commented, almost as though she could hear his thoughts.

That wasn't possible, was it? He knew some creatures could do such a thing, but not with vampires. Besides, she was human. He was at least mostly certain of that.

Taking another whiff of the air, Declan could place the prominent fragrance immediately. Roast Duck. It did indeed smell delicious, however, a glance at Rosamund quickly stole any further thoughts from him.

She was looking up at him, no longer wearing a smile, but instead wore an inquisitive expression. She was studying him like one might examine a subject to be pursued, explained, and explored. She was analyzing him, looking for something. What, he did not know.

He liked it, the way she ever so slightly sucked on her bottom lip, and how her brow furrowed a touch, with her head bent to the side. She was lost in thought, lost in analysis, much like he often was. Whatever was going on in her head, it was clearly important, and he wanted to devour every thought, to know what it was she was gleaning from him.

He wanted to kiss her, to devour every sensible and analytical thought she had ever assembled, so that all she knew, all she could process, was him.

"Shall we have a seat?"

She blinked for a couple of seconds, remembering where they were and registering his question. The hold on his arm tightened, and he feared that she might pull away, but instead, she tucked herself closer to him.

"Yes, sorry. I was—"

"Lost in thought, yes. A common occurrence for most academics. Never fear that you are alone in such endeavors. I find myself lost in thought far more often than one would normally care to admit."

She did not speak again as they were seated at a small corner booth, separated by the table. Declan had been reluctant to let her go, and she had paused a half second too long before releasing him to take her seat, but there was no other way about it.

It would seem as though conversation would not abound over dinner.

"I must apologize, for I had not expected the space to be so loud. I fear our conversation may be lacking if we are forced to struggle to hear one another."

Rosamund shook her head at him as she wrinkled her brow, a smile curling over her lips all the while. "The pleasure of your company will make up for the lack of conversation, and besides, we cannot talk while we eat."

"And yet, I would prefer the sound of your voice to any meal they could place before me."

The words had slipped past his lips before he could help himself. But they were, apparently and thankfully, the right ones, given how her pretty blush was once more spreading over her face. He was stopped, however, from making another compliment by the arrival of their server.

At that very moment, Declan knew he was, in fact, in trouble.

in which an invitation is made

Rosamund smiled at Declan, trying to bring a smile to his lips as well, but it seemed impossible. Their server arrived and began listing off the daily specials, including the roasted duck she had immediately ordered. Their appearance seemed to set his mood off rather foul. Whatever the server had done or said...

Declan now refused to meet her eyes and was instead glancing down at his lap.

Did he have a cell phone down there he was hiding? She doubted it. Something about him made her suspect he didn't have or use a phone. And besides, she doubted he would be so rude. He had wanted a conversation, so why was he now avoiding it?

"Are you all right?" she voiced, wary of his answer.

"Mmm," he murmured as his gaze finally lifted to hers. His eyes were dark, so very dark, and the lines across his forehead were... concerning. He was tense and seemed to be uncomfortable as well. "Yes, my apologies. I have... my head. It comes and goes at times, I'm afraid. It's very loud in here, and seems to have triggered it."

"Oh, should we—"

"No, no," he said, cutting her off before she could offer they leave. Good, it might've meant an end to their evening. "I will become accustomed to it soon, I hope. Please, I know I am... not myself at the moment, but I would rather suffer through the pain than lose the pleasure of your company."

He kept saying that, the pleasure of her company, as though *he* were the one who was living out a fantasy and chasing a dream.

Should she tell him she knew his secret?

No... not yet. It was too soon. And, not here. Although she didn't really know where it would be appropriate.

"I would much rather concentrate on hearing you than listen to the drab conversations of those around us. In the bookstore, you were about to tell me more about yourself, which I had hoped would include your areas of study and expertise. Please, I beg of you, tell me more about yourself, and do not hold back. I wish to know every detail."

Talk about herself? That, she could do.

Smiling, Rosamund used both hands to brush her hair back from her face, some of the shorter front pieces having slipped from the hair tie. It was all slipping, but she doubted redoing it at the table would be appropriate. Normally, she hated adjusting her hair at all, but it was giving her a moment to sort herself, and her thoughts.

Right. Everything. Areas of study and expertise. Very well then.

"Well, if you're asking me if I began more as a student of history, archaeology, or science, or the pursuit of being a librarian, I regret to inform you that my love for the preservation of books has a rather simple origin. You see, when I was younger, I would often find well-loved books in second-hand stores which had seen better days. So many of them, I often ended up reading and loving so heavily, they fell apart. And while others might simply purchase a new copy, I instead taught myself how to rebind the books, making repairs as needed."

"Ahh, so you taught yourself, and eventually decided to pursue archival work professionally?"

"Sort of," she answered with a smile and blushed as she looked down at her lap. How could she… she had to be careful, of course, because if she gave too much away… "I actually read a book about various kinds of hand stitches throughout the ages, and became more interested in the different kinds. Before that, I had been relying on essentially glue and cardstock, but once I began to understand how the assembly all works, and how each step has a purpose, and how different stitches—I'm sorry, I know this is likely boring to discuss."

She had to get off this topic before she gave too much away.

"Anyway, I did the traditional route of studying history, of course, for both my undergrad and graduate program, always volunteering and working with the library and with researchers. It was pretty well known within the community where my passion was, and I was offered a position upon graduation. I've considered pursuing my doctorate, and I took a variety of library science classes along the way, but I enjoy what I do, and…"

He was smiling at her, his head no longer bowed. Whatever was affecting him must have ended. He was now fully engaged with her, his posture much more relaxed. She smiled back, having now lost her entire train of thought. Right, classes, her degree, and…

"You, Rosamund, are a wonder," he complimented once more, bringing a blush back to her cheeks.

Dammit and damn him. She was not a woman to blush, and yet he was forcing her to do so every few minutes. She felt like a schoolgirl with each one, which was absurd because she was a grown-ass woman in her thirties, who knew what a fucking amazing person she was, and she was not the sort of woman who blushed over compliments.

"And, do you still repair your own books at home? Those you've read so many times that the spine is cracked?"

"I do," she answered with a smirk, shifting a little in her seat. "Although more often than not, they are not books I have broken from use, as I take care of my things, and I tend to have multiple copies of the same well-loved books. No, my repair work is now often used on older copies of books I already have."

"And what is the oldest book in your personal collection?" he asked, leaning forward slightly.

He was asking, for real. Because he was interested. He was...

Was it getting hot? Why was she flustered? Was he next going to ask how many bookshelves she had, and how full they were?

Was she turned on by this?

Wait, of course, she was. She was a bookworm. A book hoarder. A book dragon. A library troll. She was a bibliophile.

And the man in front of her loved books as much as she did.

"I have a few from the 1600s, but I wouldn't consider a book's age to determine its worth. I instead prefer to find copies of books I myself enjoy."

"And do you enjoy reading about housekeeping?" he questioned, his eyebrow quirking slightly.

Rosamund blinked, slightly confused. Why was he... oh! The book he had purchased on her behalf. The one she had been holding simply because of the binding itself, because she would then have a reason to speak to him. The one she had picked up because it stood out from the others, and she could be in the way, and—

"To be honest, I hadn't really intended to buy it, but the shop was closing, and a book was in my hands, and you... you..."

She pressed her lips together, unable to find the right words. Honesty would likely be best, but something about it felt too vulnerable. She didn't want to give away too much, and yet...

Why not?

"You make me feel flustered," she admitted, her blush once again spreading. She was going from hot to cold constantly, making her question if menopause was about to set in. "I sort of panicked, and... yeah."

"Flustered? I make you feel flustered?" he questioned, leaning forward slightly. His smirk had grown, and she could just tell he was thinking something... *naughty*. "And do you think the blush across your skin does not affect me? Does not make me wonder if the color goes below the collar of your buttoned up shirt, or if—"

He cut himself off as she sucked in a gasp, her heart now pounding. That was... he was... *naughty* had been the right guess.

He would be right, and she was so willing to let him see.

"Forgive me, please, for my words," he said in a rush. She looked up just in time to see him straightening, his eyes cast onto the table between them. "And... forget them as you consider my request."

"Your request?"

How could she forget his words, when they made her all too aware of how constricting her clothing now felt?

"Yes. Well, an invitation."

"An invitation?"

"I must apologize, again, for I am doing this all quite out of order. Given your love of books, your passion... excuse me, we shall stick with the word love—"

"It's a passion," she agreed, leaning forward, eyes wide. What was it, the invitation? Was he... no he couldn't... but was he?

"Your passion, then."

He raised his eyes to meet hers, and she could almost sense he was imploring her, begging without even speaking. What was he inviting her to do?

It took all her willpower to not lunge across the table and demand that he speak.

"Would you like to see my books?"

Rosamund blinked as the words rolled over her. Would she like to see... his... his books? Was this a serious question? Was he for real right now?

"Your... books?" she repeated, trying to be certain she had understood him properly.

"Ah, yes, you see, I have an extensive collection I've gathered over the years, and..." He trailed off as he continued to stare at her, now uncertain of himself. "If you're not interested, or if that's too forward, then—"

"No, yes, I—"

Their server appeared suddenly beside the table, setting plates between them. The motion forced her attention to leave Declan for a moment, giving her a chance to reset her thoughts and settle her nerves. She barely even looked up again as the server asked if he could bring them anything else, then left them alone once more.

"If you'll—" he began while standing up, but Rosamund rushed to cut him off, before he could apologize, or say something worse, like take it back.

"Yes," she answered, probably louder than needed. Still, she repeated herself more quietly a second time. "Yes, I would *love* to see your book collection."

"You would?" He was still half raised from his chair, half bent forward over the table, his eyes wide. He looked surprised, and then elated, his smile growing quickly. It fell just as fast, however, as he continued standing up and stepped away from the table. "You would. Excellent. But first, I must—"

"Of course, whatever you need to do," she agreed, nodding in agreement. He was tense once again, and the lines on his forehead hinted that the pain had returned. "I'll be right here."

"Please, begin eating without me. I promise to return momentarily."

He gave her one last nod before heading towards the back of the restaurant.

Rosamund watched him as he strode through the space, his shoulders tense and his fists gripped at his side. The pain had to be unbearable, given how quickly he moved. Even so, he looked back over at her one last time before he headed down the hallway, a curl of a smile appearing in the corner of his lips as their eyes met.

She could have sworn, had anyone asked, that his eyes were black.

in which a meal is enjoyed

Declan was going to sink his teeth into that fucking server's throat and drain every last drop of that fucker's life from him. He didn't even need that much blood to sustain him, and yet, he would still wash the streets with it, refusing to allow the man to return to his presence.

To return to *her* presence.

Because while Rosamund had been blissfully unaware, somehow, of the other man's gaze, Declan could not focus on anything else. The bastard had been staring at her, had been *studying* her. At first, Declan hadn't known what to think—she was a beautiful woman, worthy of attention and praise, and adoration. She was breathtakingly graceful in her movements, from the way she brushed hair behind her ear, to the way her fingers stroked the spine of a book. Any man would be lucky to be worthy of her smile, to see the way her blush spread, to receive her laughter.

But then he saw the way the man's gaze had lingered, how he had *leered* at Rosamund.

And fuck, if that hadn't made Declan ready to surge up from the table and snap the man's neck immediately.

Eyeing her like she was some sort of possession that he would take by force, like he would rip apart her blouse and force her attention onto him. Declan had seen men like him over the centuries, men who took without asking, who considered others to be something they deserved without consent, and he...

He treated them now as a vampire much as he had in life, with a force that only a forceful man would recognize.

By taking, demanding, and spilling their blood.

Not that, by any means, Declan was a good man. He also took by force, took the blood of humans, took their lives, and yet...

He needed their blood to live. This man, this beast, this server, he wanted Rosamund simply because he wanted her.

Because he thought he had the power to do so.

But Declan knew what genuine power was, and he was going to show the shitbag as soon as he tracked him down.

Luck was on his side as Declan followed the server's stink out a side door, to a dark alleyway. Two men were standing together, with one putting out a cigarette and stepping back in through the doorway they were leaned against. The loud noise coming from within as the door opened and shut told him it was the kitchen, and when darkness returned to the space, Declan focused in on the man.

Yes, luck was truly on his side, for now he was alone with his next meal.

There was no introduction. No grand speech. No explanation of actions. Not even a simple hello.

For such things would be wasted on a man who would soon be dead. Should there be a maker on the other side, they could easily explain why he was dead.

Declan had a beautiful woman to return to. He would not waste a single second more than he had to on his next meal.

Rushing forward with a supernatural speed, Declan grabbed the side of the man's head with one hand, and his shoulder with the other. He shoved the man back against the wall, then onto his knees, bones cracking from the use of his supernatural strength. The server cried out in pain, but Declan heeded him no mind, knowing the venom in his teeth would give the man a bliss he did not deserve in a few seconds' time.

Oh, but if only he could make this painful by choice, he would do so in an instant...

His teeth elongated as the sound of rushing blood filled his ears, the pounding of fear in the man's chest accelerating. He could smell the cigarette smoke, a stink he detested, but focused instead on the metallic blood underneath the man's skin. The scent of fear hit him as well, a pleasure Declan enjoyed, given the circumstances, and then he was leaning in, sinking his fangs into the man's throat.

He might have missed the man's jugular on the first puncture on purpose...

Warm blood surged into his mouth. The rapid pumping of the man's heart created a steady stream down Declan's throat. It was thick and luxurious, a flavor which only a vampire could truly enjoy. He felt the man's life, his soul, ooze out of him. After only a few seconds, Declan knew he should pull away if he wanted to give the man any chance of survival, but he maintained course, knowing what his end goal was.

He wanted this man dead, never to look at another woman again.

To never look at *her* again.

Rosamund.

She was perfect in every way, with her soft, doe eyes, her full and supple lips, the way she smiled at him, the way she trusted him, the way she lit up when he complimented her, the way she blushed at him. And how she had responded, when he had slipped, allowed his inner nature to betray him, mentioned having *her* for dinner, mentioned the *blush* traveling beneath her collar.

He could smell it rolling off her, the *desire*. She desired him, and he desired her as well. His very blood craved her, craved to know her. He wanted her body under his, and over his, and he wanted her in his library, among his books, in front of the fireplace, and in his bed. He wanted her wearing his shirts, with the front pulled tight to accommodate her breasts. Wanted to tuck her hair behind her ear as she read, to touch her cheek to gain her attention.

He wanted to hear her high on his venom, to hear her soft sighs of pleasure which only he could give to her. He wanted her blood on his lips. Wanted to share the blood of his conquests with her. He wanted—

He wanted her as his companion. Wanted her by his side for all the days ahead. Wanted her as she was, right in this moment, preserved for all time.

It was only centuries of experience that allowed him to remember to drag his teeth across the front of the man's throat, so it looked more like it had been cut than the bite of something... not quite animal. Those centuries of experience also allowed him to effortlessly move back so blood did not stain his clothing. Thank goodness for both, for now his mind was well and truly distracted, caught on that final thought.

Rosamund, a vampire. His companion. His queen.

He could gift her every book in his possession, could build and expand his shelves, could assist her in acquiring new pieces of art and finery, and he could dress her with the trunks abandoned in his various rooms, waiting to be preserved or worn. He had so much wealth, so much he never cared for, trinkets he had picked up through his travels, various gifts as well. She enjoyed preserving and archiving, he could give her that. Give her everything.

In exchange she would have to give up her life, but perhaps his offering would be enough?

He had never before considered taking a companion. Not truly. Not a certain person. He had longed for companionship, once or twice, and often found it with other supernatural for a short time, but he always returned to his solitude. No one could ever understand his obsession, as they described it, with his books and his library.

As more and more were turned over the centuries, too many took things such as learning and literacy for granted. As knowledge was lost to time and civilizations fell, he found the companionship he craved within the written word. They could call it an obsession. What did he care what those who became so corrupt with blood lust thought of him? He had his books. His collections. His libraries.

And now he had someone he could share it with.

If she would say the word, he would give her everything.

Licking the last of the dead man's blood from his lips and fangs, Declan straightened himself, checking his shirt for stains he knew were not there. He had to make an impression, a good one. His library would do the heavy lifting, but it was one thing to offer a bibliophile a library, and another thing entirely to ask to take their life. She would have to give her consent, and he would have to prove himself worthy of her, worthy of her time and companionship.

There could be another. Could be a human out there she loved more than her books. It was rare, in academia, that they found some-one who understood them, but it was possible. Perhaps she had reli-gion, which would hold her back. Or fear of the unknown.

It was possible she would say no, that she would have some moral quandary about living from the blood of others. And if that were so...

He would lose her.

Ah, but he could taste her, just once. Taste her blood and her flesh, and then let her leave...

No. She would know his true nature before he stripped her bare, would know the truth of it all.

He would have all of her, freely, with knowledge, or he would have none of her.

Yes, the library would do the heavy lifting, but he would charm her. Seduce her. Win her over to his side.

"You look like you're feeling much better."

Declan blinked as he realized he was no longer standing in the dark alleyway but was now standing beside the table. Rosamund was smiling up at him, her plate barely even touched. She had a book in her hands, which was utterly unsurprising. She closed it before he could catch any words and tucked it away before he could read the title from the spine.

"Much. A little fresh air does wonders for the senses."

And the blood of someone who had pissed him off.

"If I remember correctly, I told you to go ahead and eat without me."

"And I decided to wait," she answered with a smile. She gestured to his seat and plate across from her, and he took it while quirking an eyebrow. He liked that. Liked how he had been, not forceful, but encouraging, and she was headstrong. He liked that a lot. Liked that she would do as she chose, even going against him.

He had put a little *weight* behind his words, and she had fought back. Interesting.

"I'm glad you're feeling better," she said while cutting into the duck breast, and he did the same. "I was worried that our evening would be cut short, if you were feeling unwell."

"Nothing would keep me from showing you my library, if that is your concern," he teased, pausing with his food to focus on her. "There is nothing I want more than to watch you peruse my personal collection."

Rosamund's lips quirked into a smirk before she took a bite. She had looked at him just before her lips closed, and he could see the mischief in them, could see some naughty thought run into her brain, but then her eyes were closed and she was humming around her bite. The sound was magnificent. She was magnificent. Enchanting. Dazzling.

The sound sent the blood rushing from where it sat in his throat straight down to his cock.

It was going to be a long meal.

And then, he would take her home.

in which they peruse a library

"I must warn you," Declan urged as she took the turn he had already directed her to. She was driving, as he had walked into town, and she didn't want to leave her vehicle parked in the bookstore's parking lot overnight.

He was shocked she had even said that. Insinuated that she would be spending the night with him. His only response had been a quirk of his lips and a nod.

A night with him. She was doing it.

Which was why she was the one driving them back to his home.

"Warn me?" she questioned, not glancing away from the road. "Are you about to tell me that there aren't any books to be seen?"

"Oh, no. There are quite a number of books," he laughed beside her. She could almost guess there were wrinkles around his eyes as he did so, the laughter being so genuine. "In fact, it is so large a number, I fear I must warn you, to prepare your expectations."

"I'm expecting a lot of books," she teased, wanting to ease whatever fears he had. Was he nervous about what would come *after* she looked at his books? "So, you saying it's a large number is not a warning."

"Whatever your expectations are, they cannot even begin to match," he cautioned, his voice now serious. "Whatever number, whatever size... I fear you cannot even begin to comprehend the number of books I have within my collection."

"Then I shall have to spend more than one evening perusing them," she answered as she turned down the dark road he had indicated, lit only by a single older-style lantern.

Warn her about books? About the number of books? She was an archivist, used to exploring catacombs filled with books. Nothing could surprise her. Whatever number he thought was *large*, she had explored and seen more. Would it probably make her irrationally jealous and keep her busy for hours? Most likely, but she would enjoy every moment of time spent with him.

The trees on either side of the dark road began to open, revealing the home at the end of the road. No, not a home.

"This is not a house," she squeaked as she put her foot on the brake, uncertain where to even park. There was no garbage, no parking lot. Just a loop. Was there a front entrance? Of course there was, but was that even the entrance they would use? "This is a mansion."

"A manor house," he corrected. "As it sits on a large estate, complete with other buildings and residences. I own quite a large piece of land, although I have mostly left it to the wild in recent years. So much of the earth has been overly developed, ruining what was once luscious forests and fields. I prefer to keep my estate as such."

"A manor house," she repeated, staring up at what she could see with only the moon to guide her. "Uhh, where should I park?"

"Oh, you can park right in front," he answered, and gestured to the bottom of a tall staircase that seemed to rise into the sky. "There's a side entrance beneath the stairs which I prefer to use."

"Uh, huh."

All thoughts completely evaporated out of her brain, leaving Rosamund to park using muscle memory rather than with any sort of intelligent thought. When he had said she could peruse his home library, she had assumed a small bedroom and perhaps an office. Maybe even some modest shelves through the living room. A library, which would then lead back to his bedroom...

Why hadn't it dawned on her that what he considered to be a home library might be vastly different from what she considered to be a home library?

While she was constantly searching out any empty spaces on her bookshelf, often stacking books two deep, with a growing pile on her long-abandoned desk and bedside table, that was not the norm for most people, even those with a love of books. She doubted most people would understand how her kitchen table had been sacrificed in favor of becoming a workstation for repairing and recovering books. Most people didn't have stacks of books in various corners, and instead somehow held themselves to a reasonable purchase level. Not that there could ever *truly* be a reasonable number of books a person could limit themselves to.

But Declan, with his literal manor? If he didn't have a library to rival that of every great university she had ever set foot in, she would be disappointed.

Rosamund climbed out of her car and stared up the front steps in awe. A perron, they would be called, given that this was a manor house. With only the light of the moon to see by she could note architecture indicative of a Romanesque style. Things were too rounded and curved, from the pillars out front to the arch over the front door. This house, this *manor*, could be nothing else. Gothic was pointy, Renaissance was always about symmetry, and there was not enough glass for it to be Baroque.

But what was a Romanesque style manor house doing this far out in the middle of nowhere?

"So, it's big," she finally commented, staring up at one of the towers. It was enormous. That was the only word she could find for it. "It's huge, right?"

"Do you mean the library, or?"

Declan's warm voice came from behind her, causing Rosamund to freeze. She hadn't even noticed him walk around the car, nor that he was behind her. Should she look over her shoulder at him? If she leaned back, would she be in his embrace? If she turned around, could she—

"Come. Let's get you inside before you freeze. The night is growing colder with every passing moment."

Rosamund shivered as Declan touched just inside her forearm. Layers of fabric were between her skin and his fingertips, and yet, it was absurdly sensual and intimate. The way he could so easily direct her with just a slight amount of pressure in his touch, leading her towards his home, it was insanely attractive.

She had a very limited experience with ballroom dancing, having only taken basic classes while in middle school, but she thought he could easily lead her through a grand dance with just a flight of his eyes and the press of his fingertips against the back of her hand, her lower back, or...

Her cheeks burned, which she could thankfully blame on a sudden icy wind, but not for long. Not once they were inside.

Library. She needed to think about the library. The likely enormous library. And his enormous tower.

"I can hear you thinking," Declan commented, his voice nearly as warm as the air rushing around her as he opened a side door with an archway and curvature that confirmed her suspicions on the Romanesque style. "You are worrying yourself over nothing. I will not rush you through the library. You may spend as long as you wish."

Okay, so he couldn't *actually* hear her thoughts, which was good. For as much as she was trying to think about the library, she was caught up in a thousand other thoughts.

Primarily about what was big. Very big. Oh, for the love of everything holy, she needed to stop thinking about big things.

"Now, I must once again prepare you for something unfortunate," Declan murmured as he led her through dark halls.

He flipped light switches as they walked, the switches themselves often hidden or tucked away in secret panels. It was all a blur, the ambiance and decor too much for her to take in all at once. If one was to turn this place into a museum, it would fit in right away, every piece something out of a history book. A film crew would lose their minds in such a place.

"Unfortunate?" she asked as she watched another set of sconces spark to life with the flick of a switch. So much modernity in a place that spoke of ancient history.

"Yes. You see, I was not expecting a visitor to my library, and so I fear the space will be a bit chilly for you. I will, of course, light the fireplace immediately, but such a large space will take time to warm to your needs."

"Hmm," she commented, her eyes stuck on a tapestry hanging from a wall. She couldn't see all of it, the light not quite reaching as far as was necessary, but she could almost make it out. It was tickling at her brain, the name of it. "Is that—"

"It is not a remake of any tapestries you would know of," he answered before she could find the exact name. It wasn't a remake? Was it an original of— "The styles are similar, but I have had each of these made over time. I do not prefer tapestries with religious origins. They're all so... grim."

"You have tapestries made *for* you?" she questioned in wonder. How was... how could...

"Mmm, yes. To fit my tastes."

This was... too much. Far too much.

"But should you explore my manor, I must again issue a warning."

"You seem to be doing a lot of that," Rosamund said, cutting him off as she looked up at him. "Warning me. Preparing me for unfortunate things. And yet, nothing thus far has been anything of the sort."

Declan paused outside of a set of large double doors, with two wall sconces lit on either side. They were the only light in this hallway, making his face appear darker than she remembered it. So dark, in fact, his eyes were nearly black.

"Very well then." He was quiet for a moment, and she could see the words churning in his head as he found the right ones. "A confession, then. This manor, it is far larger than I require, and so much of it goes unused. My personal space, the library, my bedroom, they are the only areas which I frequent, and so yes, much of this manor is made to fit my needs, without much decor beyond."

"I can understand that," she teased slightly, grinning. "My place is basically a bed and books... or things to assist my books. Desks, shelves, all covered in books. So—"

"So you understand me, then," he whispered, his voice dropping low. "You understand..."

Her eyes closed at his words, the warmth of them vibrating through her. She understood him, yes. Or at least, she hoped so.

"And now, one last confession," Declan murmured. Her eyes opened to look up at him, just in time, as he pulled away from her. "If you will allow me... I have never shared my library with anyone."

"Never?"

"This is... an intimate experience for me, and so I must ask a favor."

"Of course." She practically breathed out the words as her heart pounded in her chest.

"Wait here a moment, so that I may start the fire and turn on all of the lighting. Then, once I return, keep your eyes closed as we enter. I shall help you in. I would like to see your face, when you see everything."

She nodded before finding the words in her throat, answering a yes, and smiled at him as he nodded in response. His fingers brushed her cheek, an intimate gesture, and she leaned into him, just as he pulled away. He opened one of the doors, a sliver of light following him, but it did not give her enough to see beyond the first few inches. He slipped within, leaving her to stand in the hallway, a shiver running down her spine.

This was... she was...

Rosamund took a deep breath, trying to slow her pounding heart. This was the wildest, craziest, most dangerous thing she had ever done. All of it, from seeking him, to finding him, to dinner with him, to now being at his place, his freaking *castle*. It was insane. She was insane.

And yet, he was about to show her an expansive library, one which he had never shared with anyone else. She felt like freaking Belle from *Beauty and the Beast*, and the child in her, the one who knew every word to every song from the animated film, leapt for joy.

The woman in her was pressing her thighs together, trying to remind herself that showing off his library was *not* a form of foreplay...

Okay, no, there was no point in lying to herself. This was definitely foreplay.

How long was it supposed to take? How long was she supposed to wait? She shivered again, still waiting for him, half considering opening the door despite his request and her agreement. When the door opened before her, he slipped out quickly, not allowing her to see within.

A smile was on his face, and she shivered once more, although this time not from the cold.

"Now, as we agreed?"

She nodded before closing her eyes and covering them with her hands. It was like a dream, like a fantasy, as he led her forward, one hand on her hip. She nearly leaned back against him, wanting more of his touch, craving it, but she wanted to move into the library.

Touching could happen *after* she saw the books.

A door closed behind her, and then he pulled away, leaving her alone. She could hear crackling in a fireplace nearby and smell the woody smoke, a bit of warmth reaching her as well, but beyond that... She waited, hands still over her eyes, keeping her from seeing the treasure she knew was all around her.

"All right," he told her, finally. "Open your eyes."

Allowing her hands to drop at her sides, Rosamund took in a deep breath before finally doing as instructed, opening her eyes. She immediately noticed the warm welcoming of the space, from the glow of the fireplace to the depth of color on the shelves to even the various furniture. Where other rooms and halls had all been dark and gloomy, this area was all well-lit, with a variety of wall sconces and lighting from above brightening the room. Even the loft above was well lit, and the area below it...

The loft, the balcony, the second level above, were all open. The rolling ladders, the stacks going from floor to ceiling, reaching as tall as the manor itself, were all building and flowing around and around. Stacks were sitting in neat rows on the floor, waiting to be organized. Stacks of books on desks. Books open on a table. Books upon books, upon books upon...

She felt faint, everything overwhelming as she turned, trying to look at it all. Thousands upon thousands. No, hundreds of thousands. Even that felt too weak a number. The number of books, amount of learning, the possibilities, were all of it endless. There were books with matching leather bindings, a set of collections to be certain. Books purchased within the past year, the spine revealing modern and contemporary titles. She wanted to touch them all, to run among the stacks. She wanted to ride across on the ladders, to climb up each of them.

"I am never leaving," she breathed out as she turned, trying to look at it all, but still finding more books with every turn of her body. "I think... do you just purchase every book that is released each year? You must. This many books... I mean, I don't know how many published works there are in total, but you might—"

"There are duplicates," he assured her, not that it was of any real assurance. "Particularly when new editions are released. I also have a penchant for a variety of covers. In fact, there are at least three dedicated shelves simply to the work of Tolkien. As you said before, there is a hobby for collecting books."

A high-pitched giggle escaped Rosamund as she turned again, not even knowing where to look. This was... she was...

Oh, for the love of God.

"I am never leaving," she repeated, still not looking at Declan. She was in love. In love with this library. In love with this space. All she needed was a warm cup of tea, a good blanket, and some fuzzy socks, and she was sold.

She was never leaving.

"That can be arranged," Declan murmured, a tease she had to assume, but she wouldn't argue with it.

"A book can take you somewhere," she quoted as she tried to pick a place to start. Where could she even start? Was there a proper place? Should she ask him for a tour of the shelves? What was his organization strategy? Did he follow any pattern? "A bookshelf can take you anywhere. A library can take you everywhere."

She was never leaving. That was final. She was just going to live here, in this space. She was—

"What did you just say?"

"Hmm?" She turned, almost startled by how forceful his words were. His eyes were wide, and he approached her quickly, too quickly. How—

"What did you just say?" he asked again, his eyes searching hers. "Have you heard that somewhere, or?"

"What... I'm sorry, what did I—?"

"A book can take you somewhere... a library everywhere. Have you heard it somewhere, or...?"

"I'm... I read it somewhere," she answered, blinking up at him.

Shit... fuck... oh fucking... had she just—

"Why?" she asked.

That was right. She had to put it back onto him.

Because the answer was, she had read it from one of his books. Would he admit it? But to admit to such a thing, that would mean confessing so much more...

"Do you not agree?"

He had to admit it now. Had to admit the truth. Had to admit who he was.

Anything else would be a lie.

in which he admits a few things

Declan was not one to know panic or fear.

In his waking life, in his human life, before the supernatural had become reality, and before he had become one who walked with the night, death was simply a fact of life. Death was all around him. Death was a simple reality.

If he fought hard, trained hard, and worked hard, then he would survive, until the day when he simply could not do enough. Could not be enough. And then, he would have his eternal rest, safe in the hands of the Gods.

Life had been simple.

Then, a vampire entered his existence and changed him. Transformed him. No longer was he a farmer, working on his land. No longer was he a soldier living from his pension. No longer was he the third, a name that he grew to hate with time, for it revealed his place within the world.

No. He became something more. Something to be feared. To be respected.

Something with time. Immortality granted him so much time.

He did not fear death. Did not fear pain. Did not fear the unknown.

And yet, this woman with wonder in her eyes and pages of books written into her skin, gave him fear. Made him panic. Made him... concerned.

Because what if she didn't like his library? And in turn, what if she didn't like him?

Fuck, to be worrying over a woman... a *human* woman...

In his human life, companionship had been found only among his animals, and among his brothers in arms. Married life, a wife, children, they had never been in the cards for him. He was a third son, with nothing to inherit, nothing to his name, simply a piece of land that he worked diligently on. His personality and his good fortune had come once he was a vampire, and by then, he had his books, and his research, and his learning, and his travels. A woman was for...

A woman was for worship, yes, but not for companionship. They wanted riches, they wanted security, they wanted children. All things which he could not give them.

Because, for as much as he saw value within knowledge, it was not enough. And as kingdoms and empires rose and fell, security was always lacking. And children were something an immortal could have for but a moment, only for them to fade away with time.

But this woman... this *human* woman...

She saw value in books. She saw security in knowledge. And he had a sneaking suspicion, given the current age where it was becoming more and more socially acceptable for women to become something beyond a mother, that she might be far more open to the possibility of never having children.

There was hope in their connection. And that made him afraid.

Because for the first time in a long time, loneliness was pressing at his very soul.

With supernatural speed he would be unable to explain to Rosamund, should she go against his request, Declan moved around the library, turning on every switch, bringing the space to life. He so often worked in the dark, having no need for lighting to see, or at least with only a little lighting, that he was unprepared for the beauty of the space once it was fully lit and viewable. Would she like it? Would she enjoy it?

He could not sit and ponder the question, for the fireplace also needed to be lit. He no longer required warmth, and only lit the fireplace for ambiance. It was a good thing the wood was dry, for he would be ashamed and unable to explain if it did not catch quickly.

He would have to change things around the manor if she stayed. If she stayed human... if she refused him....

A fear he could not consider at the moment.

He wanted to view his prize. Wanted her to view his gift to her.

A human... a woman... another being. He was sharing this with her, his most secret and precious treasure. Years of gathering and collecting, all sitting in one space. And here she was, a being who also saw value in it. A person he could share with. A woman he could...

Love.

If such a thing were even possible for a vampire.

As Declan guided her into the library, he took a single glance at her throat, watching as she swallowed, and then held her breath. How would she respond, if he dragged his lips across her skin, licked at her throat. What would she do if he nipped at her?

He shouldn't think about such things, for fear that he would give into his lust.

Lust. Not blood lust.

He might not know if love was possible, but lust was abounding.

"Open your eyes," he instructed, and watched as she did as instructed, first lowering her hands and then opening them.

And just like that... his question disappeared.

The wonder in her eyes expanded, and she held her breath as she turned, taking it all in. The warmth and light of the fireplace made her glow, and he watched as her eyes widened further, heard the intake of breath as she finally remembered she had to do so, and felt the pounding in her chest rattling against his own. She was beautiful, ethereal, and she was in his space, in his personal space.

He would have her in front of the fireplace first, and then on the couch, and then he would carry her to his bedroom where he would continue his worship, having her body contorted and alive in so many ways which only he could give her.

And then, he would turn her immortal like himself, so he could preserve her, just like this. So he could keep her perfect.

She would forgive him one day. Forgive him for turning her into a monster.

"I am never leaving."

That could be arranged.

Time stood still as he watched her, watched as she tried to look at everything, as she tried to take it all in. Pride swelled within him, knowing that she was amazed, that she was pleased. She was happy, smiling, even giggling to herself. She was... perfect.

And now he had to make his move. Somehow. Some way. He needed... something.

"A book can take you somewhere," Rosamund said suddenly, her head tilted to the side. "A bookshelf can take you anywhere. A library can take you everywhere."

Declan froze. He knew those words. Knew them in his heart. They were words he had spoken a few thousand times over the centuries, as he had explained himself to his fellow immortals in regard to his passion and his collection. He had even written the words down a time or two, in some of his books. Some of which were published.

Now, a true panic set in. How could she know his words? Did she... No. She couldn't. Of course not. He was careful. He always changed his name between genres and generations. Not even those he worked with knew of his true nature. She could never. Of course not.

When was the last time he had uttered those words onto paper. Recently, surely. Yes. It had to have been.

There was no other explanation.

"Do you not agree?"

"You know that I do," he answered, still staring at her. When had he moved so close? Why did his fangs feel ready to extend, to attack?

"I do," she agreed, nodding her head once. "Because they're your words."

So, she knew. Knew his secret. Or at least one of them.

How much did she know? How much *could* she know?

"You knew who I was, when I entered the bookstore," he finally concluded, still staring her down.

It had been a trap. But, for what purpose.

Surely, she couldn't... she wouldn't be stupid enough if she knew everything. So then—

"I did," she confirmed, staring him down. He waited to smell fear, to see it in her eyes, but she didn't flinch. Didn't pull away. "Although I was surprised you hadn't used your pen name to introduce yourself."

Right... Of course. Because Declan wasn't his pen name. Or at least, it wasn't this century.

"So the meeting," he said, taking a step back. "You planned.. . what?"

"I don't know," she answered with a shrug after a moment. She wasn't lying to him, he could tell that much, but she was still keeping something back. "I just... I wanted to meet you. Your work on repairing leather book covers was what set me on my path to archival works. Finding your mystery novels was entirely by accident. It was only because of your use of the same phrasing that I was able to piece that together. I have—"

"You know about the mystery novels?" he questioned, taking another step back. How many... how much she did—

"I have a sneaking suspicion I've also read one of your fantasy novels. That one was a bit more work to discover. A book on dragons, without a series? It was only because I went looking for it, that I was able to find it."

"It wasn't my best work," he confessed, and shook his head. So, she knew about his published books. "Is there *more*?"

"*Are* there more books?" she asked, raising an eyebrow at him. "I've certainly looked for them. You used different pen names and have no social media presence. There's no connection at all, save for how you word things, and your use of the same publishing house, not that you have many options. I'm surprised, though, in this day and age, that you are using a publishing house. You would have far more control should you independently publish."

Was she giving him publishing advice now?

"I must confess that I am now, myself, at a loss for words," he uttered. "I had never guessed, or assumed, that anyone would ever..."

"That's okay," she said with a smile. There was mischief in her eyes as well, and that brought a whole new level of panic to him. "You sit and think about what you want to ask me next while I explore your library."

The little minx. First, she leaves him confuddled, and then she tells him to sit and think while she explores his space?

This was a woman worth keeping. A real prize. A researcher. A bibliophile.

She was a wonder. But he had to know more.

Rosamund was now wandering along the wall, not touching, simply looking up and down, taking it all in. He watched as she continued her perusal, not stopping her exploration. If he had to guess, she was making a mental map of the space, which was admirable, except he had lost track of his organization a few centuries earlier.

He would have to fix that as well.

Following along behind her, Declan said nothing as he took her in, took in her body, and the way she moved through his space. She was alluring as her fingers trailed across one of the rolling ladders, and when she glanced over her shoulder at him, he shuddered, unable to stop himself from drowning in her eyes. He had already known her to be an attractive woman, a woman teeming with sexuality and sensuality, but now that he knew he wanted her, craved her, he couldn't stop himself from wanting more, needing more.

And to know that she sought him out... that she enjoyed his wor ks...

She enjoyed his works, right? She had pursued her career based on one of his books, but she had never said anything further.

What if she didn't like his work?

What if she didn't like *him*?

The fragrance of her sex rolled off her suddenly, and he froze. All thoughts left his head as he focused on her, on what she was doing, searching for what would cause such a reaction. She was aroused, excited, and he had no idea the cause of it, or how he should respond. He couldn't comment on it, of course, as she didn't know he would even be aware of such a thing, but he had to say or do something. Perhaps urge her along?

Her walk continued, and like a helpless puppy, he wandered after her, his eyes wide as he continued to breathe her in. If she was *trying* to increase her essence, he would believe it, the scent of her so strong. If he sank to his knees before her, he would find a treasure trove beneath her skirt.

Would she allow him such liberties?

"I enjoyed the fantasy book, by the way," Rosamund said, cutting off whatever bit of brain power he still had left. He focused on her again, on her neck in particular, as she turned back to look at him. He watched as she swallowed, and then heard it, heard her heart pounding rapidly in her chest. If he didn't know any better, he would think she was enjoying him following her, perhaps even entertaining it. Almost like he was a predator, and she was his prey.

That wasn't too far from the truth.

She turned back around, her gaze seeming to return to the shelf, but she didn't take a step forward. The bookshelf she was looking at was all reference books which were surely outdated, so he doubted she had any actual interest in them.

Was she waiting for him to respond? Or was she waiting for him to do something?

Because if they stood there much longer, with the scent of her sex flooding his nostrils and the pounding of her heart thrumming in his ears, he was going to sink his teeth into her throat while working his fingers into her cunt.

In that order.

in which she plays her hand

He didn't know. He had no idea she now had the upper hand.

Letting it slip that she knew he was an author of several books hadn't exactly been as she planned, not that she really planned much. More like... imagined. She hadn't imagined it going quite like that. Really, she had assumed he would charge at her, reveal all of himself with his anger. Or, perhaps, that he would deny it all.

Instead, he had stared at her in wonder and confusion.

And he hadn't realized he gave himself away.

Because the book in question, the one from which she had quoted, without meaning to, the one she had mentioned as her inspiration for her career aspirations...

She would guess, if she had to, that he was about thirty-five. Maybe forty.

The book she had mentioned was published over eight decades earlier.

Which confirmed all her suspicions.

He was immortal. And she wanted that immortality.

It had been clear, the moment she stepped into the library, that she was making the right choice. All these books, so many untold treasures, it would take ten lifetimes just to open them all and read the title. She needed that time, needed that immortality.

And him. She needed him as well.

But broaching that subject, broaching any subject, felt impossible. She had just revealed that she knew what he considered to be his deepest secret. At least, the deepest one she could possibly know of. Because things like immortality? That was impossible. A scientific feat that had never been accomplished. It wasn't real. Why would she, in his eyes, ever suspect such a thing?

Not only did she suspect it, but she now knew it to be true.

Should she instead bring up the attraction she felt for him? Somehow, that felt even harder.

Not because she didn't know he was attracted to her. That much was obvious. The way he studied her lips, held onto her arms, stared her down, he was clearly besotted with her. And why wouldn't he be? She was beautiful, intelligent, and loved books in the same way he did. She was probably a dream to him, particularly given how alone he seemed to be.

Immortality with books sounded amazing, but not having good sex or someone to share a book with? That would be lonely.

She was his dream come true, whether he realized it or not.

But she was also already half in love with him. And somehow, revealing that felt hardest of all.

"You only enjoyed the fantasy, then?" he questioned, sounding a little unsure of himself.

Her eyes focused once more, no longer lost on the leather bindings of some encyclopedias that had seen better days. Declan had sounded concerned. Was he worried she hadn't enjoyed his books? Had she completely misrepresented herself?

"Declan, please," she scoffed, fighting the urge to look over her shoulder at him. If she did, she might *actually* embarrass herself. "You're an excellent writer, both in terms of fiction and non-fiction. I selected my career based on one of your books. I sought you out based on your books, which is... kind of creepy when you think about it."

"I'm flattered," he corrected, but she shook her head. No. They needed to at least address her less than legal research methods. Because, uhh, what she had done was *mildly* freaky.

"I connected that you were the same author of multiple pen names across multiple genres and tracked you down because I was half in love with your books. You completely changed my life. Your love and respect for repairing older manuscripts literally shaped my career path. And as for your mystery novels, I'm not even a big fan of mysteries, and yet, I have every single one on my shelf. Again, I tracked you down, wanting to meet you. You don't find that the least bit creepy?"

She finally turned to look at him, crossing her arms under her breasts as she stared him down. She had tracked him down! That was weird! Normal people found that weird, so why didn't he? This had to be an immortal thing. Or maybe a loneliness thing.

"You're a researcher," Declan corrected, then took a step closer. "You're the kind of person who sees a thread and starts to pull at it, unraveling it. How interesting that you say you do not enjoy mysteries, and yet, you sought to solve the mystery that is my identity."

"It's morally wrong," she pointed out. "And again, possibly stalker behavior."

"If I hadn't invited you to dinner, or invited you here, would you have returned to the bookstore, seeking me out again? Would you have followed me to my home? Tried to force our paths to cross again? Broken in to see my library?"

He was only two steps away now, so close that she could reach out and touch him. So close that he could reach out and touch her.

Would he, if she asked? She suspected so.

She had thought he would grab her by her throat, demanding answers for how she knew so much about him. She was almost sad he hadn't. Although maybe he still would, once she revealed all of his secrets.

Okay, no, bad train of thought.

"Tell me what you're thinking," he murmured as he took another step forward. His eyes were dark, nearly black, reminding her of how he had looked at the restaurant before stepping out because of his headache. When he had returned, he had been rejuvenated, practically glowing.

She was lost in those dark eyes now. Lost in wonder of what they meant.

Of what he would do next.

"Tell me the truth. Would you have continued following me around and seeking me out?"

"No," she confessed, then licked her lips. It was the truth, she realized. She had simply wanted to confirm her suspicions, but if it hadn't panned out she wouldn't have pushed it further. "I just wanted to know if I was right... and meet the man whose books I was in love with."

"*Was?*" His eyebrow quirked at the word, and she blinked, watching as he took another step towards her. He could touch her now, if only he lifted his hand. She could easily do the same. "Are you saying you no longer love my books?"

"I..." She felt almost drunk, or drugged. She was lost in his eyes, unable to pull away. She was melting in front of him, her knees ready to crumble underneath her. She couldn't blink, couldn't move. She knew the answer to his question, and yet she couldn't voice it. What was he *doing* to her? What was he *going* to do to her? "I..."

He blinked as he turned and moved away, showing her his back. Rosamund took a deep breath as she stepped away as well, blinking. What had he done to her, that she was so lost in him, unable to move or pull away? Was that what the darkness did? Was this one of his immortal abilities?

"I apologize," he began, but she rushed to cut him off.

"Yes, I'm still in love with your books. With all of them. And your library."

He turned to look at her, but said nothing more, did nothing more. The distance between them was a chasm, and she wanted to cross it, to cut the distance and the separation, but she feared it. Feared the intimacy of it. Feared that what she might say next would make him pull away and cut her off entirely.

"I sought you out because I thought you would understand me, and my love of books, but beyond that, you were a mystery I had to solve. You shaped so much of my life, even pushed me outside of my normal reading spaces. I mean, you could write a book on how to change tires, and I would probably read it."

He scoffed, but she continued all the same. She wasn't entirely too far off.

He had written a book about historic forms of wagon and carriage building, after all.

"And then you invited me to dinner, and appreciated my love of books, and my work. You were interested. Do you know how many guys are interested in a girl who spends her days covered in paste and stitching new spines and—But you were interested, and then you invited me back here, and showed me the most amazing library, which I never want to leave, and Declan, I'm—"

He was still staring at her, unmoving. His eyes were no longer black, but now the color of oiled leather, like a book. He had seen so many things, done so many things, knew so many things. He was like an encyclopedia, and she was ready to delve into his pages. She just needed to open herself up to the possibility. To ask him if he was open to it as well.

"I'm... maybe a little in love with you as well. I don't know. But you can tell a lot about a person by their bookshelf and their book collection, and what I can see here is a love of literature and knowledge, and preservation, and art, and it's something I've never found matched in another person, ever. The way you care for these books, the way you write, the way you—I never want to leave this place."

He took a single step toward her as soon as she went silent, then stopped, as though holding himself back. He stared her down, but his eyes were not dark as they had been earlier. What was the difference now? What was he thinking?

"Truly? Be certain of how you answer. Would you truly never want to leave this place?"

He was leaning in towards her, but still not stepping forward. The distance between them no longer felt like a chasm. Instead, every step that kept them apart felt like a rope she needed to balance across to reach her end goal.

Here it was. The opening she had been waiting for. The moment she had craved.

It was time to play her final cards. Time to raise her bet. Time to win the game.

Rosamund stepped forward, not looking away as she closed the distance. He didn't move away, but he did straighten up, no longer leaning in towards her. His eyes widened, as though surprised, and she smirked, feeling like the cat about to catch the mouse.

Not that this man was a mouse. If anything, he was more an unassuming predator.

She would love to be his prey.

It was only as she stepped in front of him that she realized she didn't have an actual plan, other than revealing her final card. She had no idea what to say, or how to even begin. There was no gateway, save to repeat the word *forever*, but that wouldn't say *enough*.

"Would you want to stay?" he asked again, his voice full of wonder as he stared down at her. She liked it. Liked their slight height difference. She could lean into him and feel his lips on her forehead easily, or perhaps go onto tiptoes to kiss him. She could do that. She could—"Would you stay forever?"

Her lips quirked again, the only sign that she now had her entry point. There it was. Perfect.

But for the love of everything holy, she desperately wanted to kiss him.

She kept herself from crossing that boundary. Not just yet. Not until the card was played, and he knew what game was afoot. So instead, she reached up, and brushed her thumb across his bottom lip. He shivered in front of her, and she waited for him to gasp, or to catch his breath, but he did neither. Instead, he continued to stare, the question still clear in his eyes.

All she had to do was answer.

"The only way I can stay forever is if you make me immortal, like you."

And there it was. Her final play.

in which our predator chases his prey

One moment, he was under her spell, seduced by the look in her eyes and her essence in the air. She was aroused, excited, and approaching him. Her fingers brushed his face, his lips, and he had shivered under her touch, the intimacy of it overwhelming. He was more man than vampire before her, and while her blood was still a drug he craved, he desired her as a woman far more.

And then, the next moment...

An immortal. She wanted him to make her immortal. Like him.

Not a vampire. Immortal.

She was so close, so very close to the truth. And yet, so far away.

The minx. He couldn't even begin to guess how she had even figured out that he was not entirely human, but for her to think he was beyond death, without realizing he was in fact a form of death...

"You published your last instructional guide on book repairs more than sixty years ago, Declan. You also reused some of the same phrases in two earlier versions, as far as I've tracked down. At first, I thought it was plagiarism, but then I realized everything about the way you curated words—"

"I've published four books on the matter, actually," he corrected. He hadn't pulled away, and neither had she. She was still staring up at him, her eyes wide, questioning, smiling. She was pleased with herself.

And she should be. She had found him out. Not only had she discovered his various names, but to also discovered his secret, and to track him down...

By all the gods, this was a woman to be reckoned with.

"Impressive," he complimented, not looking away from her. "A job well done."

She practically beamed as her smile widened, and he noted how she enjoyed praise. In fact, she seemed to enjoy praise for her researching skills and work far more than him complimenting her appearance.

But now, he had to correct her.

Her fingers left his lips to trail to his jaw, and he tensed, a moment of fear passing over him. She had sought him out for his books, yes, but also for his immortality, or at least, what she thought was immortality.

Was that it, then? Was this the true reason she had sought him out? A desire for immortality? Nothing more?

If that were the case, he would have changed her regardless, if for no other reason than amusement, but this woman was...

He focused on her eyes, studied her gaze, and lost himself in her depths. She was breathtaking. Perfection. She possessed the kind of beauty men had fought wars over. Had she been alive a few hundred years earlier, every renaissance painter in every city would have longed to have her sit for them. He would have been the envy of every party and celebration he ever attended, with such a shining jewel on his arm. She was magnificent.

And she was smiling up at him with far more than just hope in her eyes.

Anyone could tell a lie, even to a vampire who wasn't expecting there to be a lie. But some things couldn't be faked. Some things couldn't slip by a vampire. Like the way her heart was racing, and how her gaze kept flicking to his lips, and how her sex was flooding his nostrils. She desired him. She *wanted* him. And the way she had spoken about the books, the passion with which she held for them…

His fears were absurd, because while Rosamund *did* want her immortality, she also wanted *him*.

And perhaps she could have both.

There was still one thing she was missing.

Declan grinned at her before turning his head towards her hand. Her palm curled against his chin and over his mouth, and he forced himself to keep his lips closed as he breathed her in. He could smell the last traces of their dinner, but he could also smell ink, leather, paper, and all the things he found fascinating about her. It would be the greatest loss of his life if he could not keep her.

But she had to know the truth.

"Do you know the cost of immortality?" Declan murmured against her palm before turning his head, so she was once more touching his cheek. Her eyes were closed, lips parted as she took a slow breath, but she opened them again to look at him. "Did you know that it comes at a cost?"

She moved her head to nod, then shook it. Ahh. So, she had assumed there was a cost, but she did not know what.

"Tell me the truth, how you figured it out. The order of it all." He was careful not to increase any part of his vampire aura. He had slipped a few times, and each time she had nearly frozen while her body sent off waves of desire. Her desire for him was so overwhelming that when she was forced to lose her inhibitions, to reveal her true self, she was seemingly sent into what he could only label a panic.

He didn't want her panicking now. He wanted her to answer him.

"I found your book on repair work first. The most recent one. It was… probably twenty years ago," she whispered. Her fingers brushed over his cheek, the intimate touch making it difficult to keep his eyes open. "Your mysteries I found in high school, but I didn't realize it was you, not at first. It wasn't until the sixth one, where they solve the mystery because of the—"

"The clue tucked into the spine of the book, yes, very good," he confirmed, nodding his head. He wanted to keep urging her on, and to maintain the warmth she was giving him as long as he could before he possibly destroyed the moment. "And then?"

"And then I began university, and I read the repair manual from the early 19th century, and from there it all began to unravel. I couldn't stop thinking about it. Made it my mission to find out more. I realized there was a pause in your mystery releases, and searched every book released from your publisher in that time, wanting to find if you had published something under another name, finding the fantasy. And then—"

"Yes, I was stuck in my next mystery novel. It was an absurd notion."

"I still enjoyed it," she breathed out.

She wasn't looking away from him, entirely focused. She was waiting for something more.

Very well then.

"Your research was excellent, and your theory panned out to be mostly correct. I'm very impressed," he complimented. She bloomed under his words, and he gave her a moment to enjoy it before he broke her a little. "But you see, I am far more than immortal."

He waited for her to respond, but all she did was lick her lips, and that nearly fucking broke him, because those lips were meant to be kissed. To see them swollen from kissing, and from his attentions. And he would soon, very soon, see them dripping with blood as well.

If he was lucky.

"There is a monster behind this mask, Rosamund, for immortality, which I do have, comes at a cost. A bloody and deadly cost."

Before she could panic or turn away from him, he moved, faster than she could have imagined or ever prepared for. Her hand, which so tenderly cradled his face, was now caught, with her wrist held tightly in his grasp. His eyes darkened, as they did when he was insatiable, and his senses enhanced as well, her lust now threatening to overwhelm him as he sucked it in. And his fangs, the things she should fear most, elongated, ready to make her his next meal.

"You see, I am far beyond immortality, my dear," he growled around his teeth. His voice was deeper like this, rougher. "I am the monster in dark shadows, who sinks his teeth into the innocent, draining them of their life and their soul. I am one with the night, unable to ever bathe myself again in the light of day. I feel no warmth, require no food, and yes, I have immortality, but the cost..."

He did not look for her reaction, wanting instead to drive home his point. If she had fanciful ideas about him, of what she could have, of what she could be... being a vampire had its gifts, yes, but it could also be a cruel existence, if one were not prepared for it.

He knew the cost before he was turned, and even then, it had shocked him to his very core.

Lifting her wrist to his mouth, he fought the urge to bite her, and instead licked her flesh, his tongue dragging along her pulse. He could nearly taste it, could feel it against his touch, and he let himself lick again, this time adding the drag of his fangs. He didn't pierce her, not yet, but he craved to.

"Even now, even with as much as I want you," he continued, his voice still deep. "As much as I crave you as a woman, crave you naked beneath me and over me, I crave your blood even more. The desire to drink from you, to devour every drop of you is... overwhelming. And this is even after I have recently fed, for I drank from our server this evening while I stepped away."

He still didn't look at her. The man in him wasn't prepared to see her fear. Not while the vampire was in the lead, enjoying discussing his last conquest.

"He kept looking at you with a lust and desire in his eyes, and I knew immediately his intentions were far from pure. The sort of man who wanted only power over a woman. I didn't even try to stop myself from draining him dry, and I did not need to eat. My lust for blood, and for the power it gives me, was too much for me to fight. Not when he dared to look at you like that. Not when you were sitting across from me like a deity I longed to worship. It took control of me, forcing me to take his life."

He still held her wrist, but his mouth pulled away as he looked at her, leaning in. He wanted her to see his teeth, to know the danger in them. He wanted her to realize the situation she had placed herself in, by trusting him. He needed her to know the cost.

"That is the cost of immortality. The curse of it. It is far beyond anything you likely could have imagined. And for as much as I want you, want you beside me, crave to have you, to give you pleasure, I—"

"I want that."

He froze at her words, unable to continue speaking.

"I want that," she repeated. Her eyes were wide, and he could feel how tense she was, but she wasn't pulling away, and there was no fear. No, all he saw in her eyes was wonder, and desire.

She still desired him. Even after his threats. Even with the danger.

Magnificent, divine creature.

And she was soon going to be all his.

His grip on her wrist loosened entirely, allowing her arm to drop. He knew he should say something more, give his list of demands, before he would do such a thing, but before he could even find the words, she was suddenly turning away from him. For a moment, he feared she would run, that it was all a lie, but instead, she casually *wandered* away from him, still taking in the library.

What on earth was she doing, and why was she walking away from him?

He went to follow her, to demand an explanation, when she glanced over her shoulder at him, a smirk once more on her face. There was a flicker of something in her eyes, a tease, and he realized what she was doing. Or at least, he hoped she intended to be doing such a thing.

Because he had just revealed himself to be a predator, and she was fluttering away like his prey.

Every instinct in him demanded that he chase her, catch her, trap her. He could do it, of course. Demand her attention be returned to him.

But what was the fun in that?

Oh no. Right now, he much preferred the idea of stalking his prey.

Rosamund turned away from him as she reached a spiral staircase. He moved behind her, stalking silently, and reached the bottom step just as she reached the top one. He didn't look up, for fear of seeing what was beneath her skirt without permission, but followed her trail like a hound on the hunt.

He was so focused on everything about her, about the racing of her heart and the slowness of her steps, and the way her scent floated towards him, that he nearly missed her question. She was lingering near an assortment of old maps, something he knew she would enjoy, given what humans now knew of the world, but she avoided it, confirming what he already knew. This was a chase, not an exploration.

Right. Her question.

She looked over to him, expectantly, and he shook his head, trying to piece the words together.

Would she truly be able to stay forever?

"If that is your wish, then I would never make you leave," he confirmed, not moving from where he stood at the top of the staircase. If he moved any closer, he would pounce, and this was a conversation that was actually important. "You should know that we will always be bound to one another, should I turn you, although the bond will lessen with time, if we part ways."

"And leave this library behind? I think not."

She winked at him, winked! and then continued down along the shelves, her fingers brushing over several spines. It was as though she was marking them with her scent, and he was left to follow once more, stalking his future companion.

"I'm beginning to think you only want me for my library," he commented idly, struggling to maintain the distance between them. It was getting harder, the more they moved. Apparently, he was not very good at stalking.

He was a little too old to be playing with his food. Not that she was food.

"Declan, please," she scoffed, and looked over her shoulder at him again. She was near a blank area of wall, which he would eagerly push her against so they ruined no books. Although he suspected she would just as likely enjoy being fucked against a bookshelf. "I love your books, and I love your shelves, and I love your library. It would be so easy to love you."

Love. She had said it before, so casually, so easily.

She darted away from him, quicker than he had expected, particularly given the little journey she had led him on. They hadn't made it far, only a few minutes of walking, but for her to randomly dash...

The demand to chase took over, and he darted after her using his supernatural speed. In an instant, she was in his grasp, her chest pressed against a shelf and his chest pressed to her back. She was breathing hard, although he doubted it was entirely from the running, and he leaned his head in, breathing the scent of her hair, of her shirt, of her throat.

She whimpered as his nose brushed where her collar met her skin, and he growled against her jaw, his inner monster demanding to be freed.

Soon. She only needed to agree...

"I will turn you on three conditions," he drawled against her temple before dragging his lips over her ears. She was ripe, succulent, supple, soft in his embrace. He hadn't truly held her yet, hadn't really felt her against him. With so much of her body covered in clothes he was ravenous to see her true form. To see every delectable inch of her soft body. So very soon...

Her response was more breathy moan than actual words.

"Anything."

in which the prey is properly seduced

A vampire had her trapped against a bookshelf, his body pressing against hers, and all she could think was that her underwear was soaked, and she really hoped he took them off soon.

Anything. Anything he wanted. Anything to maintain this feeling. She would do it. Anything.

The cost of immortality was drinking blood? She was not some innocent fool who didn't know bad people existed in the world. It wouldn't be too hard to drink from them. Of course, she would have to get over the idea that she didn't know where her food had come from, or where it had been, but that was what mouthwash was for.

And if immortality, vampirism, meant she could keep Declan, keep this library, keep these books...

Vampires were real. A vampire. He was a vampire. A monster of old lore.

And she was unbelievably horny because of it.

It probably made her a terrible human, being turned on by a monster who had stalked her through his library, and killed a man for having ill intentions for her, but she wasn't going to be a human for much longer.

Anyone who wanted to judge her could take it up with her need to feed.

Declan's hold on her loosened only long enough for him to turn her around. She expected to feel his body press against hers, something she could only dream of up until that point, to feel his leg pressed between her thighs and his chest against her breasts. She wanted to kiss him, was desperate to kiss him, to lick his fangs now that she knew they existed, to allow him to taste her blood. He craved it, so of course she wanted him to have it. Wanted him to have every inch of her.

Instead, his hand went around her throat, holding her there, tight enough that she couldn't move even an inch away from the wall, but not so tight she couldn't breathe.

She noted the way his focus locked on her lips, and she licked them slowly, then caught her bottom lip with her top teeth, worrying it slightly. She wanted him to feel as desperate to kiss her as she felt. Wanted him unable to resist whatever urges were overwhelming him.

"The first condition," Declan began, reminding her that they were in fact having a somewhat important conversation about her future. "Is that I must drink from you, now. You should know what it is like, to feel your blood being drawn from your veins, and I shall need to do so to turn you, so—"

She lifted her wrist to his mouth almost immediately, ready for him to do so. Bite her? She might have a thing for that anyways. And if he needed to do it to turn her, she would gladly suffer a little pain.

But Declan's reaction was not what she expected. Rather than sinking his teeth in, tasting her, he released her throat and took a step back. She didn't know what instinct took over her, because it certainly wasn't any desire for getting away from him, but she smirked at him before ducking away from his arm and dashing further along the walkway, careful of the nearby banister.

It would be cruel and ironic if she fell from the second floor, dying before she could become immortal and truly explore this paradise he had presented her with.

There was a gust of air, telling her what she already suspected was about to happen, just before it did. His hand wrapped around her forearm, stopping her from going any further. She didn't want to, of course, nor did she have any intention to fight, but the desire was suddenly there all the same. She struggled against him, still grinning as he grabbed her other forearm.

He backed her up against a shelf. She turned her head to see what it was he had her pressed against, when she saw a familiar woman's name, her eyes widened.

"Careful! Is that an original print of—"

"You're testing my control, Rosamund," Declan growled as he pulled her away from the bookshelf and then pushed her back against a small section of wall. Thank goodness for all the lighting around the room, creating empty spaces between the shelves. "Next time you dash, I don't care what book it is, I will have you against it—"

She laughed, feeling brattier by the second, and his eyes grew darker as he lifted her wrists against the wall, holding them above her head. She was unable to pull away, trapped, nearly going onto tiptoes from the movement. She was stretched out in front of him, and he loomed over her, somehow seeming bigger than he truly was.

She was unable to look away, not that she even wanted to.

"My second condition is that you must drink from me, before I turn you. You will have to drink my blood regardless, to be turned, but I want you to know what it is like to suck the essence of life from another. Granted, it will be mostly your own, after I have just—"

Rosamund whimpered at the thought of doing so, sharing blood with him. Something about that sounded so viscerally intimate, to share blood with a vampire, her blood, or to be a vampire and share between them...

To any human, it should sound absurd. Possibly illegal. And yet, here she was, turned on at the thought of doing so.

Declan took in a deep breath entirely through his nose, and when he looked at her again, his eyes were no longer black, although they were certainly dark. His gaze moved down, towards her breasts, and then lower. Could he smell that? Could he smell her desire?

"As a vampire, are your senses better?" she questioned, wanting to know if it was possible. "Because the way you keep breathing me in..."

"Good girl, yes, I can hear better, I can taste better, I can see better. I can move better, and yes, I can smell how soaked are. Although, I shouldn't call you a good girl, given how bratty you've been, running away from me."

She whimpered at his words, unable to keep it to herself, and parted her lips, licking them again. He seemed to like that before, and now she was desperate to kiss him. Desperate to taste him. Desperate to move beyond whatever cat and mouse game they had been playing all night.

They were both going to win, both going to earn the prize. The game was over. She just wanted *him*.

"What is your final condition?" she asked, her voice sounding far steadier than she had initially expected. Particularly given how her heart was pounding so hard, she was pretty sure she was vibrating.

He looked into her eyes, his own gaze still dark, but his fangs not elongated. He was more man than vampire, if she had to guess, but waiting on the man to speak was agonizing. He was simply staring at her, not responding.

His gaze moved lower, downwards, and she followed him, watching as he lingered on her throat, and then to her breasts. She felt constrained like this, with her arms above her head, and she tried to arch her back, but it was useless. Declan had her trapped, to do with as he pleased, and while that thought excited her, she was also growing impatient.

He was edging her in the best and worst way possible, because the second he touched her, *touched* her, she would combust.

"Do you know how ethereal you are, just like this?" he questioned as his gaze lifted to meet her own. "Your beauty is beyond any comparison, but if I was forced to place you into any box, I would call you Rubenesque. The softness of you, the curves of your body, of your breasts, of your backside, and lower. Every part of you is voluptuous, even your perfect lips. You are truly a work of art."

Her lips parted at the mention of them, and she took in a shuddered breath, waiting for something more. What did her beauty have to do with his final condition?

"Your intelligence as well, and your dedication to research. You have a mind which is unmatched, save perhaps for my own. Our passions, our desires, our drives, what we thrive on, what we enjoy... We fit together, you and I, in a way I never imagined possible."

If he was about to propose marriage, she was going to demand the library as his wedding gift.

"What is it, Declan?" she finally breathed out. "What is your final condition?"

His hands slid up her forearms to her wrists, and he moved them together. His two hands holding her became one, while the other slid down her arm, down to her collarbone, and then over to the top button of her blouse. He didn't do anything besides tug at it slightly, and he quirked an eyebrow at her.

"Please, yes, go ahead," she answered his silent request, and took in another shuddered breath as he popped the first one, and then the one below. He continued his way down but stopped midway. His hand then moved up higher, to her collar, and he pulled it aside, revealing her collar bone, and the top of her lacy bra.

Only then did his gaze move from her eyes, where they had been locked. He looked from where the last button sat, and then up higher, to her throat, before leaning forward. He took a deep breath, first at her throat, and then lower, to just above her cleavage. His reaction was visceral, a full body shudder, and she arched against him again as best she could, trying to force her breasts higher, trying to urge him to touch them.

Anything. Anything to take off the edge. Anything to allow the dam to break.

"Never before have I craved a creature as much as I crave you," Declan murmured, his voice lower in tone. When he looked up at her, his eyes had gone black, only to then return to brown. He was fighting the monster within him. "Not just your blood, nor your body, but also your mind. Your passion. I crave you exactly like this and would never wish you to change."

Rosamund licked her lips and nodded slightly, although she didn't know what she was agreeing to. Yes, craving, desire, want, need. Just like this. Just like this very moment. She never wanted this moment to end, save for their joined pleasure.

"My final condition is that if I change you, I will do it tonight. Before you can... No. I want your full consent, because this life... there is no returning to your human form, but I would also not have you talk yourself out of it. I want you to desire this, me, all of us as you do now. Preserved in this moment."

"I..."

"I will drink from you, you will drink from me, and then I shall change you, tonight, in this very room." He was listing it all together, so she could see the path entirely. Either she left this library a vampire, or...

She didn't know what the alternative was, but she desired nothing else. Just like this. She would be just like this for eternity.

Perfect.

"I have a condition of my own." Her voice was far steadier than she would have expected, given how her heart ached in her chest from pounding, and how lightheaded she was from both desire and need. "If you're... I mean, I think I speak for the both of us when I say we're sexually attracted to one another, but ignore the condition if—"

"My attraction is in question?" Declan interrupted as he leaned in. He took another deep breath of her throat, and then moved upwards, the side of his face brushing against hers. She shuddered at the almost nuzzling gesture, and felt his lips press against the corner of her ear, not a kiss, but simply present. "My attraction to you is limitless. I crave you intellectually, yes, but also carnally. I would know your body, every soft dip, every sound you make, every desire you hold."

He growled into her ear before pulling away. His eyes were once again dark, and she watched as his fangs elongated. He shook his head slightly, trying to shake them away, but he was losing the battle.

She should probably hurry up with her condition, then.

"I want you." Declan stopped moving his head at her words, and looked at her, his gaze darkening fully. His eyes were so black, she was lost in them, unable to look away. "You know I want you. Desperately. If you touched me, I would lose my mind. So, my condition, my request, my proposition, fuck—"

"Say it," he growled, leaning into her. "Tell me you desire what I long for."

"I do." He didn't have to say it. Not with the way he was responding to her. Not with the way he was surely losing a battle with himself. "If you're going to turn me, if you're going to drink from me, and me from you, then have me. Have sex with me. Fuck, that feels so lacking a word, but I want the intimacy too, I want the pleasure with the pain, I want you, I want your teeth in me while I ride you and—"

Declan's growl cut her off, and then he was surging forward, his mouth at her throat. She could feel his teeth scraping, and she arched up against him again, unable to do anything more to do the distance.

"Bite me," she begged, struggling against the bond. "Drink me, undress me, fuck me, love me, just bite—"

He did as she demanded, his teeth sinking into her skin, sending webs of pain shooting through her body, from her throat to her stomach, and down her arms, then continuing into her very soul, through every part of her being. Pleasure quickly followed, a high she couldn't chase enough, like a drug made just for her.

She screamed as the pleasure rolled over her, flooding her senses and every part of her body.

She was lost in him, lost in the joining of pleasure and pain.

And soon, she would be his for all eternity.

in which blood is finally shared

Declan had known from the start that resisting Rosamund was a pointless battle, but now that he had her in his grasp, with his teeth in her throat and her blood in his mouth, he was possessed. Nothing could stop him from drinking from her, from tasting every drop of her blood. Her life force, her essence, her very being, flowed into him, strengthened him, forced him to crave her more.

She was overflowing with lust and desire for him, and her screams were more pleasure than pain, fueling him, driving him on. He released her wrists as he grabbed her body, pulling him to her, and she moved easily, her arms going around him to cling to his back. She wasn't pushing away, but instead clung to him tighter. He knew the pleasure was overwhelming now, the pain likely having begun to subside, and then he felt her start to weaken, her hold loosening.

Too much. Fuck, he was pulling too much from her. It was painful to withdraw his teeth, but he had to, had to force himself to let go of her.

Forcing his vampiric side down, Declan withdrew from her throat and pulled back to look in her eyes. Her heart, which had been rapidly pounding before, was now slowing down, a sure sign he had pulled too much.

His teeth sank into his own wrist, and he shoved it into her mouth without ceremony, so his own essence could fill her, sustain her. Her eyes were unfocused, and he urged her on, begged her to return enough to her senses that she could start sucking. The first few drops hit her tongue, and then she grasped his forearm, clinging to him as she sucked at the open wounds.

Declan moaned, the sensation strange but sensual, something he was unused to. Sharing blood was something vampires only did in the most intimate of settings, often finding themselves too lofty to give their blood to another, given how they had to work for it. For him, however, it seemed obvious to share with her. She was his match, his equal, his companion.

He would always share his blood with her.

Her eyes opened, and he saw they were once again focused, staring back at him. Life was renewed within her, and her heartbeat picked up speed, rapid to a point of near concern. He knew it wouldn't kill her, to drink his blood, but it was like she had life in her, a new spirit. She was going to have to burn some of that off, and quickly.

Rosamund released his wrist and looked down at it, down at where she had been sucking, only to then latch back on. Declan chuckled, amused at how she was unable to stop herself. She was insatiable, unsurprisingly. He wouldn't stop her until she was done.

And then, he was going to fuck her through their shared highs.

She pulled away again, and he nearly expected her to give into her desires once more, but instead, she licked her lips and looked up at him. He licked his own lips, cleaning her blood from his mouth, and waited for her to speak, or to act. He could see it in her eyes, how they flickered about, and how her hold on him tightened, that she was processing her feelings, processing her thoughts. He wouldn't rush her on that either.

Drinking the blood of a vampire was... an experience.

"Will it always be like that?" she asked, blinking rapidly as she spoke. "The... the feeling, I mean. The rush. Is drinking always like that?"

"It is," he confirmed, and brushed his fingers into her hair, tucking a fallen piece behind her ear. He knew how that bothered her and had seen her tuck her own hair back a number of times. "It also feels that way to give blood."

"Do you do that often?" she asked again, her words still in a rush. Ahh, she was struggling with her racing heart, then. "Share blood, I mean?"

"Only in the most intimate of settings, and with those you trust. You're giving them a piece of yourself, of your very life, when you share blood."

"Will you still share blood with me, after I'm turned?" She sounded almost worried.

Declan chuckled as he nodded. "You? Always. We will always share blood. Everything that is mine will soon be yours. And you... you will be mine, in all ways, for all eternity."

Rosamund nodded her head in a jerky manner, then released his wrist. He pulled himself away from her and took a step back, giving her space. Her legs were unsteady, like a newborn deer, and he waited to see with her newfound burst of energy. He remembered the first time he had tasted a vampire's blood, just before...

Well, it had been centuries earlier. He wouldn't think of such things.

"I feel like I could fly," she breathed out, staring down at the floor. "Like I soar."

"You cannot fly," he corrected while smirking at her. She was adorable, trying to process everything, and as a little researcher, he knew she was trying to figure out the whys and the hows, and the wheres, and all the questions she was intellectually being forced to ask herself. "But you will burn off the energy quickly."

"I want to be chased." Her words were still in a rush, and she looked excited. "Do you want to chase me? I want to be chased."

"I can chase you," he agreed, his chuckle growing darker and lower. The idea of chasing her called to his vampiric nature. "Do you want me to bite you when I catch you? Or more? You should know, I will bite you when I catch you."

"I want you to undress me when you catch me," she begged, then grinned at him. "I want you to undress me, and then chase me, and bite me. Over and over again, until we're both naked."

Declan chuckled to himself as he nodded, looking her over. He would enjoy undressing her.

"And when I catch you for the last time, I'm going to devour every last drop of you."

Rosamund shivered where she stood, and he looked lower, to where her skirt covered her sex from his view. But not her scent.

"I do not mean your blood, Rosamund. I mean I will have you sit upon a throne and allow me to devour every drop of your sex. You've been calling to me all evening, driving me insane. I will taste you."

"A throne?" she questioned as she took a step towards him, and then backed away. She seemed to like the idea of that.

"Oh, yes. My jaw will be quite the throne for you. I long to feel your thighs on either side of my head, gripping me. You will always be welcome to sit on it."

A high-pitched squeal escaped her, and she clapped a hand over her mouth in shock, only to then giggle. Clearly she was too high to even control her responses. He chuckled again, and crossed his arms, waiting for her response.

It didn't take long.

"But... I mean, I don't want to smother you. You'll have to be able to breathe."

Declan chuckled as he looked down at his feet and toed out of his shoes. There was no seductive or sensual way for him to take off his shoes or socks, so he might as well get them out of the way now, before he chased her down.

"You forget, my dear, that I am dead. I don't breathe. You can sit on my face for hours, without pause, coming on my tongue until you cannot move. And even then, I'll still devour you."

She was frozen where she stood, her eyes wide, and he chuckled again. Oh, yes. She was certainly overwhelmed at this moment. Poor thing. She needed to burn the energy before he pinned her down and fucked her.

"Now, I think you said something about being chased?" he urged and nodded his head once. "Run."

She was gone immediately, turning and running away from him while he awkwardly bent down to tug off his socks. When he caught her, the first thing he was removing was her sweater, followed quickly by her skirt. He wanted to see what she was wearing underneath, how high her tights went, and wanted to see her thighs.

He needed to sink his teeth into her thighs.

She didn't get far before he charged after her, pinning her into a corner and grabbing her wrist. She fought back, a grin on her face urging him on, and he tugged off her sweater from one arm, and then the other. He moved in to sink his teeth into her throat, but she ducked underneath him, not faster than he could move, but fast enough that he allowed her to escape, to tease him.

He dashed again, this time catching her by her skirt, and pulling her body back against his. She moaned as he cupped her through it, feeling the warmth of her cunt. The skirt was too tight, however, for him to do much more than feeling the heat, and he fumbled to tug at first her belt, and then the buttons of the offending garment.

She helped him, thankfully, unzipping the skirt as he sank his teeth into her throat, using that to pin her there as he wrapped his arms around her middle. She arched back against him, and he opened his eyes to see her kicking off her shoes along with her skirt, leaving her in hosiery which went as high as mid-thigh.

Something about the idea of unrolling it from her legs called to him. He would certainly enjoy that.

His teeth left her throat, and she stumbled forward, not getting far before she half fell into a chair a few steps away from him, reminding him that the running, and his own bite, would drain her quickly. He followed her and bit his wrist, only to sink to one knee in front of her so that he could press his bleeding skin to her mouth while tugging at her blouse. The last few buttons sprung free, and she shrugged out of it, one arm and then the other, still clinging to his wrist.

He let her drink until she pulled away from him, but didn't allow her to rise, instead pushing himself up and stepping back. His shirt easily went over his head and onto the floor, and then his pants followed, his belt giving him a moment of trouble.

No more belts, for either of them. They were too much of a hassle, and he was done with the tease. He wanted her now. Wanted the lacy purple underwear, with the straps connected to the hosiery, to be long forgotten, and for her bra to be out of the way, and for her body to be his to explore, his to devour. He wanted nothing in between them. Wanted only her, for all eternity.

"Run," he urged again, and nodded towards a set of stairs, opposite the set she had run up earlier. "To the fireplace."

She giggled while doing as told, and he made a note to compliment her, to call her a good girl once he caught her again. He watched as she ran down the stairs, then across the open space towards the fireplace. She looked over her shoulder up at him, and then he was jumping down from the second floor, landing with practiced ease, before stalking after her.

She stumbled away from him as he moved forward and grabbed her by her hips, stopping her movements. He could feel the warmth of the fire, knew it was now warming her skin, and he knew it was time. Time to complete this. Time to have her. And then, time to turn her.

"I could spend an eternity drunk on your skin," he murmured against her throat as he leaned in. He didn't bite, not yet, but he did move his hands up her back, seeking out the clasp which kept her breasts covered. It was an easy thing to snap, and she shivered against him as the lace fell away. Leaning back, he looked down to see her, to see the first revelations of her nakedness.

He was right. Any painter would kill to have her naked body on display for his artwork.

"Perfection," he murmured, and shifted down to one knee, so he could nuzzle at her stomach. She sucked in, and he nipped at her belly with human teeth and not fangs, then moved lower. So close. He was so close to what he craved most. "I will return to your ample bosom shortly, but first... I'm starving."

Rosamund giggled again, and her hands went into his hair, gripping tight. Ahh, he did love that. He would have to return the favor soon.

His fingers hooked into either side of her underwear, and he pulled it downwards, revealing dark curls which glistened, soaked with her own desires. He took a deep breath, enjoying the taste of it teasing at his senses, then continued lower, pulling her hosiery with it. As they reached the floor, his hands went to her hips, helping her to stay upright as she stepped out of it.

He was still wearing his undergarments, but they were of no matter. He would remove them shortly. Her pleasure came first, so she was soft and limber and receptive to his *roughness*.

"Do not silence yourself, nor hold back," he urged, nuzzling at the top of her thigh. "I want to hear all of your screams."

His fingers parted her lips, almost immediately coating them in her essence, and she shuddered over him. He wasn't even exploring, and yet, she was already on edge. He would enjoy this. Enjoy every second of it.

His fingers pressed at her opening, two sinking in easily, just as his teeth sank into her thigh.

in which he is insatiable

Everything felt surreal.

She understood, now, why Declan had insisted on her agreement and her consent before he acted. Before, she had thought herself lost in pleasure and desire, but now that she was drunk off him, drunk from his blood, and drunk from him taking hers, she was floating, or falling, or tumbling, or something else of the sort. She thought she could fly, but also felt herself drowning. Everything was so much more intense, and yet she was also numb.

It was too much, too overwhelming. Her senses were going haywire, trying to understand what in all she was feeling. Hot and cold, hard and soft, everything a whirlwind in her mind. Even the pleasure was tingled with pain, yet there was one thing she knew for certain, one thing to keep her grounded in the moment, aware of who she was, where she was, and who she was with.

Declan was holding her, keeping her upright, keeping her safe. He was her security, her strong point. He was going to take care of her, worship her, and give her everything she had ever desired. She was his, entirely his. All she had to do was give in to her desires and let him control the rest.

So she sank into the pleasure, knowing nothing beyond his touch.

His fingers curled inside her, and she dug her toes into the carpet, trying to both pull away and sink into him further. He held her upright, a little unsteadily, but she trusted that he would keep her from dropping. He was strong and would not allow any real harm to come to her.

Almost as soon as the idea passed her mind, her knees buckled slightly. His thumb was rolling her clit, finally giving it the attention it had throbbed for hours for, and that action had her ready to pass out, the pleasure so overwhelming. His free hand moved up from her thigh to her hip, steadying her, just as his mouth left her skin. The pain of his bite subsided, leaving her only with the pleasure of his touch, and she wavered again, ready to crumble.

Before she could fall, however, her toes left the carpet, and her butt settled into a soft chair. Her head fell backward, and she blinked her eyes open to see the ceiling. Chandeliers hung from it, but beyond that, it was almost plain in comparison with the rest of the space. A simple white.

"You should have a mural painted on the ceiling, if I'm going to be spending so much time on my back," Rosamund mumbled, hoping he would understand. "Or... something. Yeah. Just. Something."

Declan chuckled darkly, and she blinked sleepily as she looked down between her breasts, the heavy, unbound things falling to either side without a bra to contain them. He was on his knees before her, her blood staining his lips, and he grinned at her as he lifted her legs by the back of her knees, spreading them with the movement and dangling them over each armrest.

"I should have a mural painted?" he questioned and shook his head slightly. "Of all the things you could say right now..."

"I could also say I want to come," she grumbled, trying to force her eyes to stay open. Her mind felt so hazy, sluggish even. "And that my eyes are heavy."

"I'm taking too much, then," Declan murmured as he kissed the inside of her ankle. "You need to drink from me again."

Rosamund opened her mouth, finding no qualms with the idea. The taste of his blood was not what she had expected, nor the texture of it. Thick, oozing, but also both metallic and yet bland. She would have to get used to that, the taste of blood.

But what she felt after the initial taste was a high she couldn't stop chasing. Her entire body thrummed to life, her senses buzzing. She was in overdrive, and the energy inside of her was intoxicating. She truly did feel like she could fly.

She liked the hazy feeling when he was drinking from her, but the way she felt after tasting his blood was indescribable.

Declan grinned at her before leaning forward and sliding his arms underneath the back of her legs. He tugged her down on the chair, so her butt was nearly falling off the seat, then lifted his wrist to his mouth. She watched in wonder as he bit into his own skin, then lifted it to her mouth. She didn't have the strength to reach out and grab him, to lead his arm to her, and had to wait as he shifted forward on the floor.

His wrist reached her lips just as his other hand moved between her parted thighs, spreading her folds. She lapped at the two holes in his wrist with her tongue, savoring the first drops of his blood, only for his tongue to connect with her swollen clit a half second later. The pleasure of his attention mixing with the high of his blood was too much. She had been edged for too long.

With a burst of energy that was only possible thanks to his blood, Rosamund reached up and grabbed his forearm, clinging to it as she drained more of him. She bit into his flesh with her teeth, not that it caused much damage, but something about it felt right, wanting to bite him in return. His teeth, or something else sharp, brushed her clit, a bit of danger tingling with the pleasure, and at that—

Her nails dug into his skin, keeping him from pulling away from her entirely while her head fell backwards. Her scream echoed in the library, echoed in her own ears enough that it hurt, but she couldn't stop. She couldn't stop screaming. Couldn't stop the waves of pleasure that were... no, not waves. It was one massive wall that she had just slammed into, all pleasure, all endorphins, all overwhelming, and corrupting her in the best of ways. All she knew was the high of him inside of her and around her. Of his blood running through her veins.

Even where he had bitten on the inside of her thigh and on either side of her neck no longer ached. All she felt was rapture, euphoria, pure ecstasy. It was better than anything she had ever felt in her life, stealing the breath from her lungs, and all the blood from her head.

She was going to die like this, die from the pleasure of him.

Rosamund's screams stopped as soon as the air in her lungs ran out, and she sucked in a deep breath, ready to scream again, only instead...

Instead, she sobbed.

The pleasure, the bliss, the overwhelming feelings and emotions, the edging, the teasing, all of it flooded her in a way she never could have prepared for. She felt so much, felt everything on edge. Her body ached suddenly, and her mind felt broken. She couldn't move, couldn't pull away. Not that she wanted to, but...

She needed a moment to breathe. To think.

Declan's mouth left her cunt before she could even speak, and she looked down at him, her eyes wide, trying to find the words. She was... it was... how was...

"You're all right," Declan murmured as his hand moved from her sex entirely, and instead began stroking up and down her leg. "Just breathe. It can be exhausting, feeling so much at once. I imagine that I will feel equally as drained once I've lost myself inside of you."

She sucked in another breath, nodding despite her tears. Right. Drained. Yeah, that was... No, that was not the right word.

"I feel everything. And it's not draining. It's drowning. It's..."

She looked down at his forearm, where her nails were digging into his skin, and she nearly pulled it back to her mouth, only to realize that the bloodied spots were now healed over. That was probably a good thing. She should have her head clear for a moment.

"Is it like this all the time?" she whispered, a little horrified at the idea. To be so overwhelmed with all her senses all of the time. It would be too much.

"At first, it can be difficult to control it," Declan answered, his honesty scaring her slightly. "But I promise, with time, it will become easier to manage. You learn how to focus on certain things. You learn how to shut it out entirely. It's only when we let down our guard and our defenses... and when there is blood."

"So, the sex will always be..." She hadn't meant to focus on that part, on just the sex, but given their current position...

"Will it always be this intense?" His eyes darkened and his fangs elongated, teasing her. She shivered a little, not out of fear or the cold, but out of lust and longing. Even with how engulfed she felt, with emotions and her senses, she still wanted more, wanted him more. "As long as we burn for one another, yearn for more, we will be unable to resist the desire to share our blood, so yes. It will always be this intense."

Her tears were now dried on her cheeks, and she took in another shuddered breath while reaching for him, reaching for his cheek. They were both still awkwardly pressed together, with his arms underneath her legs and her hunching forward to look at him, but whatever discomfort she felt was miniscule compared to the reassurance she found in his touch.

She wanted more.

Declan pressed his cheek against her hand, with his fangs still dropped and his eyes still dark. His gaze stayed locked onto her, and she smiled at him weakly, before moving her hand into his short hair. She wanted to tug him close, to ask for more, but she didn't know how to even voice it, to voice her desire, to voice wanting to step back into the flood.

His nostrils flared as he took a deep breath, and he leaned forward, but then withdrew. She knew immediately what it was—he could smell her want, could smell her lust. It appeared as though she didn't need to speak at all. She tugged his hair as best she could, given how short it was, pulling him closer.

Instead of moving closer to her, however, he leaned away, backwards, until she realized he was actually laying down, and he was taking her with him.

Rosamund shrieked as she was lifted out of the chair, only to then half tumble forward as her knees hit the floor on either side of Declan's head. His eyes were black, but she couldn't see his mouth to study his teeth. Oh no, his mouth was hidden somewhere underneath her stomach, and he was now pulling her higher, shifting her to sit on his face.

Oh, for the love of—he was serious about her sitting on his face!

"Declan!" She couldn't stop herself from giggling, too shocked from their shifted position to do anything else. "Oh, please, if you do this, I might actually die."

"Not until later," he murmured into her thigh. "Just one more, and then I'll—"

"Fuck me like a vampire?"

His eyes opened to look up at her, and then closed once more as his hands moved up to her hips. He tugged her closer, her knees rubbing against the carpet as he did so, and then his mouth was upon her, licking and sucking and lapping at her slit. He was ravenous, his tongue dipping in and tasting her, teasing her, over and over again. The grip on her hips didn't lessen, and she knew he was leaving bruises on her skin. And his teeth were certainly still sharp. Not buried in her, but they were *there*.

The danger in that only made her hotter and made her beg for more.

in which she is set free

Declan growled against the inside of Rosamund's thigh, knowing he was once more losing a pointless battle. His teeth ached in his mouth, his senses were flooded with the taste and scent of her, and if he didn't sink his fangs back into her skin, he was going to lose it entirely. He had to taste her, had to bathe himself in her, had to have her blood on his lips and on his tongue and down his throat.

He also needed to rescue his cock from his undershorts before he truly died from lack of blood flowing through the rest of his body.

But fuck, she tasted so damn good on his tongue, dripping and coming and soaking him repeatedly.

At first, she had been almost timid, which was confusing to him. Everything about her oozed confidence; confidence in herself, and her abilities. He never would have thought to place the word *timid* on his sweet little archivist.

As he continued his attention and she let herself relax, he realized what it truly was. She wasn't timid. She was exhausted. She was processing. She was overwhelmed. Drowning, as she had described it. She had been so wrapped up in her thoughts as he fucked her with his tongue and licked every drop of her essence from her slit, that she hadn't been able to relax and sink into the pleasure.

But once she had...

Her passion was limitless as she rode his jaw. A human man would be unable to keep up with her, and her fears about smothering him were not without merit. Her fingers had tugged out more than a few strands of hair as he brought her to the edge, and more than once, she had leaned into his hold on her and dug her nails into his arms.

If he was not already enamored, he would have been entirely besotted with her after what he had just experienced. She was wild, untamed, and nearly feverish as he brought her to each peak.

And every time he thought she would beg for him to stop, beg for a break, she begged for more.

He would love to give her more, but he needed to fuck her, and bleed her, and feed her, and then...

And then, turn her. Preserve her. Protect her. All so that he never had to lose her.

Hundreds of years alone, and he had barely noticed the loneliness, but the thought of existing in a world without her in it, without her presence in his library and in his bed, without her love of literature, and collections, and books, without her laughter and her smile...

He would take his final death without second thought.

It was not until he had such a true treasure that he knew what it was to live without, and he refused to return to such an existence.

He growled at the very thought, unwilling to even consider it. No, she was his, and he would never give her up. She was his to do with as he pleased, to pleasure, to worship, to share blood with. He was going to fuck her as she had asked, in the rough way vampires did, without any fear of breaking their toys, sustaining them with their blood. It was not something he often took part in, and had not done so for a few centuries, but with Rosamund...

Anything. Everything. The entire world. Forever.

All she had to do was ask.

"I can't—" She gasped, her head thrown back and her hands on her breasts, squeezing them, holding onto them for dear life. It was almost as though the swaying of her body over his as she rode his jaw somehow made them hurt, which was insane, because he certainly loved watching them move, but next time, he would have to offer to hold them for her. "Declan, please, I can't, your tongue—"

She leaned further and further backwards, and he realized, in horror, that he might have pushed too far. He had been on his back for what felt like hours, overloading her with orgasms, although he wasn't exactly the best judge of time anymore. It had been long enough, though, that the fireplace needed to be stoked, and more pieces of wood added.

He probably had pushed too far.

Using both his supernatural strength and speed, Declan rolled them over, his hands moving to catch her between her shoulder blades as he did so. One moment, she was upright and sitting on his jaw, and the next, she was flat on her back with him hovering over her. He forced himself to keep his cock away from touching her, and instead focused on her face, checking to see if she was all right.

She blinked a few times, then smiled at him. That alone reassured him that he hadn't pushed too hard, but she was still breathing hard, and her heartbeat was rapid. He should probably allow her to rest before he fucked her, even though it would be agonizing to wait any longer. He craved her, craved more of her screams, of her cries, and craved her blood. He needed to sink his teeth into her once more, needed to feel her sucking at his wrist in response.

He would never get enough of her, would never be satiated. His need was too strong.

But, rest—

"Please fuck me," she whimpered, sounding almost on the verge of tears.

It was Declan's turn to blink now, taking her in, taking in the way she was still gripping her breasts, and the way her eyes were pinched closed, and she was gasping for air. How could she want more? How could she stand more?

"I feel so empty," she continued, her chest heaving a little as she tried to control herself. "Fuck me and bite me, please. I need it so badly."

Everything he knew about humans told him it was a bad idea, to take her so soon, but he had promised himself that he would give her anything she asked. To give her the very thing his body was screaming at him to do? Easy. Done.

He very well might just fuck her to death in the process.

"Shh," he murmured, his fingers running along her cheek as he spoke, trying to soothe her. "Just like this. I will take you just like this. And when you can take no more, you will tell me. Immediately."

"I will," she gasped, her eyes opening as she spoke. "I promise, just—"

"And you will drink from me each time it is offered, to maintain your strength."

"Yes, just—"

His hand moved from her cheek to her throat, not gripping, but simply warning. He held her by it, his fingers curling around the back of her neck, and his thumb running up to her chin, then back down again. He needed her to listen one last time.

"This will not be like your human encounters," he growled, trying to resist the urge to tighten his hold on her at the very thought of her with another. Never again, for he would never share her. "A vampire does not fuck like a man. We are insatiable, can last for years, and with the sharing of blood, I could keep you like this for days. Your body will be forced to shape around me, to take me. You will cry out for mercy, and then beg for more. Your body will only know my touch when I am finished, but I shall never truly be finished with you. I will spend the rest of eternity between your thighs and in your bed. Do you understand?"

Her eyes were wide, lips parted, but she didn't speak. Instead, she gave a nod, and tilted her head backwards slightly, lifting her neck up further into his hand as she did so.

Magnificent, ethereal creature.

Declan moved himself quickly, shifting his body between her thighs and shoving his underpants down and out of the way. When his hand left her throat, she whimpered a little, a sound he noted with interest, but he needed both hands at the moment. She would have to learn patience.

Her back arched as he lifted her up by her hips and took his cock in hand. She was soaked from both his tongue and her cum, her body open and welcoming to him. There was no pretense, no pause, no build up. He had waited hours to be inside of her, and she wanted to be fucked by a vampire.

He would fuck her like a vampire.

Lined up, Declan pushed forward, filling her. She gasped, her body likely not expecting the full size of him, how swollen and hard he was, how he pulsed inside of her. Her blood flooded through him as much as his was in her, and her essence, her life force, was returning home inside of her. He didn't understand how it all worked, but he didn't need to. His body felt alive, and his cock bigger as well, simply by being inside of her. She was going to feel the same.

But he wouldn't give her much time to even think about it, or process anything. He pulled back, then pushed in again, his pace steady but not rushed, instead focused on the force of his movements.

He returned a hand to her throat, not wanting his thrusts to shift her backwards. Then he found her clit, swollen and likely tender from his mouth, wanting to push her over the edge already. As soon as she contracted around him, she would be able to take an increased rhythm.

Fucking her to death was still on the table, however.

His grip on her throat tightened as he rolled her clit, but then loosened as he pulled back. Each thrust, his hold on her increased, giving her a chance to breathe, to gasp, as he withdrew. A steady rhythm, one he intended to keep for some time, only his touch on her was apparently too much, because after no more than two dozen repetitions, he felt her fluttering around him, and then the squeeze. She choked for air, and not because of his hand, then let out a scream as she hit her high.

His fingers left her clit, likely a cruelty, but he wanted to add to it without removing his grip on her throat. His teeth sunk into his wrist, drawing blood, and he pressed it over her mouth, silencing her screams and forcing her to take what he was giving her.

Her screams silenced as she writhed underneath him, struggling as he bottomed out inside of her. He could feel it, feel how her body tightened around his thickness, but unable to contract very far. She was shaping herself around him and feeling it all the more intensely because of his blood entering her system.

He watched, waited, struggled to stay still, but he knew it was coming. Knew it would click. He maintained his hold as she swallowed his blood and struggled to do something more, to accept all of him, and then... Rosamund's eyes opened and she looked up at him, focused. There it was. His blood was now coursing through her once more, all of it earlier having been burned out. He could fuck her now. Fuck her the way she was meant to be fucked. Fuck her the way she was begging for.

His wrist left her mouth as quickly as his hand did her throat, and he pulled out of her just before grabbing her hips. He flipped her over effortlessly, her belly hitting the floor as she tried to catch herself with her forearms. It was pointless, of course, because he was going to fuck her into the carpet, and she didn't really...

Well, no, she had a choice, but she had also chosen to be fucked roughly, by a vampire, and that was how he was going to fuck her, so she had the choice to stop him. But she wasn't going to.

Not his perfect Rosamund.

Declan allowed himself a single glance at her cunt, at her ass, at her thighs. She was truly a work of art, and he wanted to drink both her blood and her sex just like this, with her on her knees with her ass in the air, so he could grip into her thighs, holding her still. He would, later, but he was a vampire on a mission, determined to ruin her for all others.

He gripped her hips, digging into her flesh as he slammed home. She cried out almost immediately, but he didn't stop, didn't even hesitate or pause. He was ravenous, his body having been patient long enough, and he could no longer hold himself back. His fangs dropped fully into his mouth, and his senses focused into overdrive as he let his guard drop and his abilities free. His hips moved faster than any human man could imagine, plowing into her, forcing her body to take his. He could feel her tightening around him, or trying to, and could feel how his cock, every time he pulled out, had to push into her contracting cunt when returned.

He could hear her cries and her gasps, but he wouldn't slow. Instead, he reached down and grasped her by her hair, tugging her upright. Her arms reached out in front of her, one going to the floor while the other reached behind her, and he let go of her hand to grab her wrist, pinning it to the middle of her back. She cried out again, this time including his name, and he focused in enough to listen, to be certain she was all right.

"Please, Declan, oh, yes, yes—"

She likely could only speak because of his blood, because anyone else would be struggling to even breathe.

His hold on her wrist relaxed, allowing her to fall forward onto both hands, and he bit into his wrist again, then forced it into her mouth. He could no longer fully withdraw, but he still maintained his speed, trying instead to fuck deeper inside of her, to rearrange every part of her lower body to take more of him.

There was no longer a sense of time, no longer a sense of anything beyond the pleasure of her body, of her cries. When she fell forward, his hands mapped her form, running along her sides, up her back, down her arms. He touched and painted her, painted her body with his fingertips, then fucked her again, over and over, and over.

And when he thought she could take no more...

He flipped her back over, onto her back, and fucked her more.

Her breasts were perfect, falling to either side, bouncing with his thrusts. He had resisted them for so long, and would spend hours worshiping them soon, but for now, they were ripe and ready for his teeth, ready for his mark. His fangs sunk into the side of her breast, making her scream out in pain, and then cry out in pleasure. He knew, with his blood in her, that it felt all the better, the high reaching another level. He drank until his fangs no longer hurt and he thought his cock might break off inside of her.

And then he sank his teeth into her other breast, giving them twin marks.

Rosamund sobbed underneath him as she weakly lifted one hand to his hair, likely to grip onto him, to cling to him. She was weak, not from the blood, but from the hours they had fucked, for surely it had been hours. The fire was nearly cold, and he knew she would not be able to take much more of him. She was still a human, although not for much longer. He couldn't break her entirely. Not until he was certain enough blood was in her system.

His teeth left her flesh and entered his as he bit into his wrist then forced his blood into her mouth. She took it, sucking him weakly, and he knew it was done. She couldn't take much more of him. She needed a moment to breathe before she no longer needed to.

"One more. You're going to give me one more," he growled around his fangs. It was hard to think, to speak, beyond wanting more of her pleasure. "Then sleep."

She nodded against his wrist, and he pulled it away, knowing she wasn't quite done. He wanted his blood to sustain her and replenish her, but not reenergize her. Not yet.

His hand returned to her throat, as it had been at the start, and she gasped at his hold while he returned his touch to her clit. She whimpered almost immediately, her body jerking, a clear sign of her overstimulation. She whimpered a yes despite how weak she was, and he touched her, teased her, pleased her.

When he felt the urge to release himself, to empty inside of her, he didn't pull himself back, slamming into her so hard he nearly feared he would break a bone inside of her. And as he thumbed her clit, pinched it, rolled it, without pause and increasing the pressure, she screamed, all the air in her lungs forced out from the movement.

His hold around her throat tightened, and when she tried to gasp for more air, she couldn't. He counted, forced himself to, then relaxed his hold, giving her a chance to breathe. She screamed again as he finally found his release.

As he slumped forward, Declan only had enough thought and presence of mind to make a mental note to stoke the fireplace and bring Rosamund a blanket. Her body was limp beside his, but he could hear her heart, and knew she wasn't dead. She wasn't fucked to death, at least not yet.

Soon. Very soon. But first... sleep.

in which a change is made

Rosamund jerked awake and sat up, startled. A blanket fell around her waist, exposing her naked skin to cold air. She was sitting on a couch, alone, her body feeling beaten and bruised. Between her thighs, she was sticky and sore, but still wanting. She was trying to remember what had happened and where she was. Everything felt so hazy, so blurred. And then... nothing.

The bookstore, dinner, a drive, the manor, and then... the library. It all flashed through her mind, and she blinked, looking around the room. The library. She was still there. It was darker, with curtains drawn and most of the lights off, but there was a glow coming from the fireplace. All of it, everything that had happened, wasn't a dream. Everything was real, which meant...

"You're awake."

Rosamund blinked as she looked towards the chair beside the couch, confused. Declan, he was real too. Well, of course, he was, given how well fucked her body felt. There was certainly no way to imagine any of what had occurred over the past few hours. Or was it days? She was uncertain about time, time of day or how much time had passed, but she knew she was hungry, and that was enough to tell her that she had been asleep for some time.

"Why are you sitting over there?"

Her voice was rough and her throat sore, a reminder of all the screaming she had done, and she swallowed hard, trying to clear out the scratchiness. Declan rose from his chair and picked up something from a table beside him. As he approached, he offered it to her. It was a mug, filled with something, given how carefully he offered it to her, and she accepted it carefully, fully aware of how warm it was.

"Mulled cider. It will help to warm you, and to soothe your throat."

She lifted the cup to her lips and took in a whiff of it, the spices teasing her. It smelled delicious, and she took a very careful sip, worried it would be too hot. It tingled a little on her tongue, but the cup seemed to be far warmer than the liquid inside. As she took another few sips, she hummed, the warmth vibrating through her throat. He was right. It warmed her up and soothing her.

She took one more sip before lowering the cup from her mouth, and then looked up at him. "Are you going to sit down beside me?"

He hesitated for a long moment, but as she shifted to sit fully upright, he did as she asked, sitting down beside her. She then shifted back over to tuck herself against him, her back pressing into his side. He wrapped an arm around her shoulders, pulling her close, and she hummed again before taking another sip of the warm cider, allowing herself to relax.

It wasn't until he sat down and pulled her close that she became aware of how nervous she had been that the spell over them was now broken, and that all the promises he had made...

"Rosamund, I have made a great misstep." She tensed in his hold, nervous, and turned to look at him. He reached over and took the cup from her hand and moved to set it back on the side table, tucked between his chair and the couch they were now sitting on. "For your see, it was only once you were asleep that I realized I had never tasted your lips."

Her nervous energy dissipated instantly, and she smiled, amused by his choice of wording. He was right. Never, in all their fucking, had he kissed her.

"I would like to, with your permission, rectify that."

She had thought he would never ask.

Shifting once more in her seat, Rosamund shoved the blanket off her and turned to climb onto his lap. Declan spread his thighs as his hands went to her hips, pulling her to sit on top of his legs. She could feel his length already hardening against the inside of her thighs, but for the moment, she ignored it. All she saw was him and smiled. Smiled as she looked down at him and stared into his eyes.

All the inky blackness of them was now gone, his eyes only brown. His teeth were short as well, no fangs elongated. He was entirely man, and if she had to guess, all their fucking had likely calmed whatever he had been ready to lose control of.

This man, this vampire, was as human as he could ever be.

"Why were you sitting over there?" she asked again. She wanted to know the answer, wanted to know if it was as she suspected. If he felt at all the same as her.

"I was afraid you would not want me beside you," he confessed as his gaze dropped to her lips. "That you might be afraid of me. That I might have harmed you. I wanted to give you space."

"I want you still," she murmured as she leaned in, her lips nearly brushing his. "I'm not afraid of you. You never harmed me. And I never want to be away from you again."

Leaning forward, Rosamund closed the distance between them, and pressed her lips to his. Her hands moved from his chest to his shoulders, and then to his neck, holding onto him as he tugged her closer. His hands ran up her back, up into her hair, and then back down again, holding her close. He deepened the kiss, his tongue teasing against her lips, and she parted them, connecting with him fully.

From there, it was easy enough to shift their bodies to allow them to continue. Her hand ran down his chest and eventually made it to his dick, stroking and squeezing him before he pulled her hips closer and lifted her up. She sank down onto his length, taking every inch of him, amazed at how well he fit. It was almost as though her body was made for him, made for this.

She kind of suspected it now was.

Declan set the pace, although it was not at all like earlier, with him nearly frantic and demanding. He had been reckless in his thrusts, fucking her in a way that no human could ever match. He had been entirely vampire, giving into his own desires and needs. Now he was a man. A man who was worshiping her with his lips and his touch.

She couldn't stop touching him either. Her hands were everywhere, from his shoulders to his arms to his chest. She stroked his jaw, ran her fingers into his hair, interlocked her fingers with his own. She couldn't stop touching him, couldn't stop kissing him. She was engrossed in him, finding safety and security in his embrace. His hands moved like hers, up and down her back, over her hips, into her hair, over and over, and over.

They were unable to stop touching. Unable to stop kissing.

Not that either of them seemed to want to.

Her first peak, although she didn't know how many she could take after what she had experienced earlier, seemed to be fast approaching, and her hips stuttered as he hit a little bit deeper while shifting them lower on the couch. Everything about being with him, riding him, it was more journey than destination, and while she was always excited for quick little stopping points, she might just die from having too many orgasms.

Was that possible? Probably not. Or possibly so. She was likely about to find out.

She pulled her lips from his, not really by choice but by necessity, and shook her head while opening her eyes. His brow furrowed as he looked up at her, searching her face for an explanation for her pulling away.

"I can't take another orgasm," she breathed out, and ran her fingers over his cheek. "I think it might actually kill me."

Declan chuckled as he pulled an arm from around her and lifted his forearm to his mouth. "Careful..."

His other hand moved to her hip, helping to move her, slow and steady. She shivered again at the depth of him, at the feeling inside of her, and opened her eyes to see blood on his lips, and his arm offered to her. "Drink. Take as much as you can manage."

She nodded while taking his arm, having to turn her head slightly to do so. The rich liquid hit her tongue, the flavor one she was now very familiar with. The first few seconds were much like before, a wave of delirious pleasure surging through her as she sucked for more, and then it spread, running through her entire system. Every part of her tingled, from the tips of her toes to the ends of her fingers. She tingled in her stomach, on her breasts, everywhere his teeth had entered her. Even her lips, still pressed to his skin, tingled with delight.

His blood was coursing through her body, his essence and life force sustaining her, fulfilling her. She was no longer exhausted, no longer unable to take another orgasm. She could take a thousand of them. Take him for hours. Take him until the end of time. She was made for him, made for this, made to be his, in this space, in this library, and in his arms. She never wanted it to end, never wanted her time or this moment to end. She wanted everything to be preserved just like this, with his taste and his touch sustaining her and fueling her.

Her lips pulled away from his skin only so that she could lean forward and kiss him, his blood smearing on their lips as she did so. His hand moved to her back, surely spreading his blood there as well, but she didn't care. Soon, her life would be nothing more than books, blood, and Declan. So much Declan. Only Declan.

Rosamund pulled away from his kiss to gasp, realizing how much more the sensations were overwhelming her. His blood fueled her senses, sending everything haywire. His kiss tasted better, his touch felt better, and her body felt so alive. She was on top of the world, ready to fly, ready to sing. She could go for hours, ride through wave upon wave of pleasure, all of it never ceasing.

"Are you ready?" Declan asked her as his hands moved, one running into her hair, tugging at it slightly.

She nodded, not knowing what he was asking, but ready all the same. Ready with him. For him. Always.

He kissed her again, pulling her close as he picked up speed, pulling her body down to meet him as he shifted up into her. She moaned into his kiss and nipped at his lips, at his tongue. He groaned and tugged her closer, still going. Oh, fuck, an orgasm, she was going to be jelly by the time he was done with her.

His head fell back, and she saw that his eyes were now black, and his fangs dropped. Was he going to bite her again, going to drink from her? She could take it. She could take anything.

"I'll be right here," he promised. "Right beside you."

She didn't know what that meant, but she also couldn't ask. Her body hit its peak, without even his fingertips on her clit. Amazing. Absolutely amazing, what vampire blood could do to her. Coming from only his cock... that was a miracle.

He kissed her again, hard, swallowing her cries, and then his hand moved around the back of her neck, into her hair, then the other hand with it, cradling either side of her neck. She kissed him back, feverish, unable to stop herself from screaming into him, overwhelmed by her orgasm.

And then, she felt nothing.

in which she wakes up

Rosamund jerked awake and sat up, startled. The blanket wrapped around her shoulders fell off, but she found she wasn't the slightest bit cold. In fact, she actually felt... hot. On fire, really. Engulfed.

Thousands of things slammed into her at once, thousands of thoughts and sensations. The couch was too rough, but the blanket was too soft. She was hot all over, while the air was cold. Her hair was in her eyes, annoying. Her body tingled all over, from her fingers to her toes, and the dull ache in her lower body earlier was now soothed.

What now ached was her eyes and her ears, and her teeth. Fuck, her teeth hurt so bad. It was worse than when she had braces in high school. They ached like something was pulling at them without any numbing. And her head... God, it was the worst migraine of her life, by far. Everything hurt, all over, particularly her neck. Why did her neck ache so badly? And why was the room spinning? And why was it so dark, and yet not dark? And why—

She nearly fell backward off the couch, only to be caught by her hips and pulled back up. She fought back against whatever had touched her, had grabbed her. A voice was there, soothing her, comforting her, telling her that she was all right, but she wasn't all right. She didn't feel like herself. She *wasn't* like herself.

Something about her felt... inhuman.

"Rosamund, look at me. Focus on me. Focus on my voice. Stare into my eyes. Concentrate on my fingertips pressing into your skin. Let yourself soak in only me. Ignore everything else."

She was inundated with sensations, all of them swallowing her whole, but she focused on the voice, on the one holding her. She could feel him, feel his hands on her, running over her arms, over her body. She tried to focus on his face, but everything was swimming.

She was drowning, but he was there, and she had to just... she had to focus on him. He was the only thing that was steady, holding onto her tight, pulling her to him.

She let herself go, allowed herself to relax, and took in a deep breath... only to feel no sense of relief. There was no swelling of her lungs, no slowing of her heartbeat...

Her heartbeat! It was gone!

A new sense of panic set in at the realization that her heart was no longer pounding in her chest, and that breathing in no longer did anything with her lungs. Everything felt wrong, so wrong, and she didn't understand, didn't know where she was, who she was, or why everything was so confusing. It was too much, and she sniffled a little as tears came to her eyes, only to smell...

Books. She could smell books. So many books.

And blood. She could smell blood.

And *him*. She could smell *him* as well.

Blinking rapidly, he came into focus, the owner of the steady voice, the one who was holding her, calming her. He was there, right there, with warm brown eyes and a furrowed brow. He was clearly worried, focused on her, and she tried to place him, tried to remember him.

She should know him. She *did* know him.

Only, he was somehow different. Clearer, crisper, but not in a visual sense, but in a... sort of awareness of his existence. Something in him called to her, telling her to kiss him. She wanted to kiss him. Needed to kiss him.

And so, she did.

Her lips pressed to his in a solid kiss, not deepening in the slightest. She didn't need to. It wasn't about making out with this man. It was about focusing on him and him alone. He was her strong point, her steadiness. He was keeping her upright, keeping her safe. All she had to do was focus on him and his kiss.

His hold on her tightened, his hands running up her back, over her sides, along her curves, and then into her hair. His fingertips brushed the sides of her neck, and like a flash, it all came back to her.

Meeting him in the bookstore, being invited to dinner, conversing about her work, being invited back to his home, exploring his library, revealing his secrets, teasing and flirting, finally giving into her desires, kissing him, straddling him...

Declan. He had asked her if she was ready. And then, everything had gone black, and she was... he had...

She was a vampire. He had turned her into a vampire.

Pulling away from the kiss, Rosamund's eyes widened, taking in his face. It was so much *more* than before. His eyes were even deeper, and his lips, she could see where they were swollen from her kiss. His teeth were not currently fangs, but she could see where they elongated, that they never really went fully blunt. She could see so much more in his face and could see now that he was certainly far from human.

And the smells... oh, the smell of books was all around them. They smelled like leather and paper and ink. She could smell the glue she had used a few days prior on a book binding. She could smell the mulled cider she had sipped earlier, the liquid now likely cool where he had set the mug. She could smell...

Oh, for the love... she desperately needed a shower... and to pee.

"Can vampires get UTIs?" she asked, her brow furrowing a little as she looked up at him.

Declan's brows rose nearly to his hairline, and then he started laughing, shaking his head. "That... I just turned you, and that's your first question?"

Her mouth opened a few times, trying to explain herself, but feeling as though she shouldn't have to. "I... I don't want a UTI! I haven't gone pee in what feels like hours, and I can feel... well, I'm going to guess your cum isn't like sperm, but I need to pee, and—"

"It's protein related, is my best guess, and no, we do not get infections, but if you need to relieve yourself, then..."

He stood up, with her still in his arms, and ran forward. She clung to him, expecting it to be like earlier, when everything had happened in the blink of an eye, but instead... If she had a heartbeat, she knew it would be moving at a snail's pace as they rushed about, as he carried her out of the library, down the hall, and to another room. She could see that everything around them was frozen, and yet they moved so fast.

Declan opened a door and raced through a bedroom, then into another door. Her butt hit a cold counter, and she yelped at the sensation, then looked down. There was a toilet beside her, thank goodness.

"I'll be just outside the door when you're ready to talk," Declan informed her, before turning and walking out of the bathroom, pulling the door shut behind him as he went.

She was alone, in a bathroom, in a manor house, with a vampire, and she was now a vampire herself...

Time to pee.

A few minutes later, feeling a little bit fresher thanks to too many wads of toilet paper and water from the sink, Rosamund finally looked at herself in the mirror, taking it all in. She looked... the same, and yet not. Somehow, she almost appeared... glittery, which was absurd, because glitter was evil, and she would never use glitter.

And yet, it was the most apt description she could find.

Her skin was brighter, clearer. But not *actually* clearer. She could still see the sun damaged spots, but they too were clearer, more crystal in her vision. Her brown eyes looked to be nearly as deep as Declan's. Her hair, she could see the grease in it, the dandruff as well. Dry shampoo wasn't going to fix that. And her teeth...

She leaned forward, studying her teeth. They were a little stained, thanks to the buckets of coffee she drank, but something about them was...

Her canines went from blunt to sharp fangs, and she gasped, startled from the pain. The dull ache of earlier was now throbbing, and she wanted to cry from how much it hurt.

"Rosamund, what is it?" Declan called out from behind the door.

She almost went to hide her teeth behind her hands, not wanting him to see, only to remember...

Right. Vampire. He probably already knew about the teeth thing.

"My teeth are killing me," she groaned, and moved to open the bathroom door. "I feel like they're—"

She froze, looking at him, taking him in. He was no longer naked, as he had been a few minutes earlier, but was now instead wearing a dark blue robe. It was tied at the waist, and he was holding another one in his hands, this one gray.

A robe. How... domestic.

"Because you need to eat," Declan said with a nod, and offered her the robe. "I am loath to cover your beauty, but this is a lot to process. This change... I tried to warn you..."

"I don't regret it, if that's your fear," Rosamund rushed to say while taking the robe from him. She didn't put it on, however. Not yet. "Do you have a full-length mirror?"

Declan raised an eyebrow at her but said nothing more as he offered his hand to her. She took it, and he led her through the bedroom into another room, this one revealing itself to be a closet. She was unsurprised to find that it was barely even half filled. He did not seem the sort to worry about clothes.

"There is plenty of room in here for your things," Declan said idly as he pulled her deeper into the space. He had a walk-in closet, and hardly anything in it. "Here you are."

He stopped them in front of a mirror, and Rosamund stepped in front of it, looking at herself entirely.

It was like seeing herself for the first time.

Much like her face, and much like Declan, everything about herself was so much clearer, so much brighter. She could see the twin marks on the inside of each breast where his teeth had sunk in, could see the marks on her neck as well, where he had bitten her repeatedly. They were faint, yet sparkled somehow even brighter.

Sparkled... almost like it was coming from within her.

"Look at how beautiful you are," Declan murmured from behind her. She watched in the mirror as he moved into view, stepping behind her and pressing his chest to her back. His arms wrapped around her, pulling her tighter to him, and his hands began to explore. "A true work of art. You will make me want to take up painting, and then I shall have to apologize every day for the disasters I attempt."

"I'll forgive you so long as you run the paintbrush over me," she teased, and smiled at them in the mirror. She focused on her fangs, still extended. They ached terribly, but she was enjoying this, enjoying looking at herself.

Even her stretch marks sparkled a little, as though she had painted them with body glitter.

"Why am I sparkling?" she asked, thinning her eyes a little. "I look like I bathed in glitter."

"It's my blood, and your blood, coursing through you," he murmured against her temple. She watched with heavy eyes as he moved his mouth to her ear, and then lower, kissing her skin. He took a deep breath of her, and she waited to hear what he would say next. "In time, it will appear less vibrant, but right now, as you're unused to it, all those with the essence of a vampire will look much the same. I thought, when I was first turned, that it appeared like starlight on one's skin. I do think glitter is a far more appropriate label."

"When were you turned?" she asked, startled to realize she had no idea. "And how old are you?"

His lips stopped their movement on her skin as he looked up at her, his eyes meeting hers in their reflection. He seemed to be thinking about it, running the math through his head.

"I am a learned vampire, Rosamund, but my gifts are in literature, not in mathematics. Over two thousand, at this point. Old enough to know that keeping track is pointless."

Over... two... thousand...

That was... much older than she had estimated.

"But, your name," she blustered, trying to explain herself. "It's Irish, from around the fifth or sixth century."

He looked sheepish and pulled away slightly, then turned her to look at him. Whatever it was he had to tell her, he was clearly embarrassed.

"Ahh, that is not... not the name I was given at birth. Nor the only name I have used over the centuries. It is simply the name I prefer most."

"Not your... Oh. Okay."

She blinked, uncertain of what she was even hearing. Not his name. She didn't know his name.

"My name at birth was Tertius Summanus, for I was a third son. I did not enjoy remembering that, and changed my name with the times, with the location. Eventually, I acquired the name Declan, and enjoyed it enough to maintain it for some time. And my last name—"

"A play on your first name," she pointed out. "Triarius."

"Indeed," he answered with a nod. "Although, it is likely time I retire such a name and assume a new one. Would you like to pick our new name?"

Would she like... *what*?

"You want me to... a shared..."

"It would only be appropriate, but I will give you time to think on it," Declan murmured as he pulled her closer with one arm wrapped around her lower back. "Women of this century often keep their own names, which I consider to be far more logical, however, it is your choice."

If she was... uhh...

"Are you proposing marriage?" she asked, raising an eyebrow at him.

Declan scoffed and leaned down to nuzzle her temple once more. "You have given your life to me, have shed the bondage of time and fragility, becoming like me, a vampire. You have an eternity now. I think what we share, our bond, goes a bit beyond the human concepts of marriage. After all, death will not be the thing to part us."

He was right about that.

"Do you regret it," he asked as he nudged her nose with his. "Allowing me to turn you, to keep you like this."

"Are you going to give me your library as a gift?" she teased, the quick remark coming to her easily. It seemed, now that she was a vampire, whatever hold he had on her before, now she was much more herself, no longer high on his presence.

"I'll give you all the libraries in the world," he affirmed, his lips teasing hers. "But first, you need to drink."

"What?" she asked, pulling back slightly. "More libraries? What do you mean? Do you have more collections than this?"

Declan shook his head as he scooped her up and carried her out of the closet. There was a bench in front of a window, the curtain closed, not telling her the time of day. She imagined it had to be daylight outside, which would explain why the curtains were drawn. He sat down and pulled her onto his lap, then tilted his head to the side.

She could see it, could see the sparkling glitter lines running over him, where the blood moved through him. Her fangs ached a little more, dropping further. A nudge of her tongue told her they were a little swollen, likely from their first time being extended.

She was suddenly so hungry. Ravenous, really. And she was ready for the pain to end.

"You need to drink, to finish the transformation," he informed her, encouraging her to do as instinct already told her. "Drink, and then we can—"

She didn't need to hear anything else.

Rosamund lunged forward, sinking her teeth into his throat. Immediately his blood filled her mouth, and she swallowed as much as she could, chasing the high, chasing the flavor. He tasted like books and mint and leather and warm tea and soft blankets and everything that made her feel safe and secure. Her gums quickly stopped aching, the pounding in her head dissipated, and the high began to run through her body.

It was so much like earlier, like before when she was a human, and yet not. Where before she had been out of her mind, feeling completely drugged, now everything was manageable. Before, her senses had been in overdrive while high, and then once turned, they were overwhelming once more, but now...

Now, it was all pleasure, all good. Everything made sense. The colors, the lighting, all of it. She could handle it. She could process it.

Pulling her mouth from his throat, she went straight to kissing him. His lips parted as he tugged her tight to him, and in seconds, they had his robe open, and her body settled over his.

She was flying, literally, as he picked her up and raced to press her against a wall. Their fingers intertwined as they grasped at one another, and he pinned her hand above her head, then ran his touch down her arm. It was good, so good, and not at all overwhelming, but instead just right. It was the perfect amount, and she lost herself in him, in his touch.

His teeth sank into her throat, and she gasped, expecting the pain, but instead only feeling pleasure. It was all pleasure as he drank from her, their blood sharing between them. And as his teeth left her throat, he kissed her again, their blood now mixing on their lips.

"I feel alive," she gasped as his mouth moved back to her throat, licking and kissing at the spot he had just bitten. "I feel... awake for the first time."

His mouth left her skin as she pushed him away from her, and then turned them around so he was the one pressed against the wall, and she was the one kissing down his body, from his shoulder to his collarbone, and perhaps lower. Declan stopped her and pulled her back to him as his fingers ran into her hair, brushing the annoying pieces from her face.

"It only gets better with time," he promised her as he tightened his hold. "Particularly now that we are together."

She smiled at him, losing herself in his eyes. This was real. This was really happening. They were vampires, and there was blood, and there were books.

So many books.

"It gets better with more libraries, right?" she asked.

His laughter warmed her before he scooped her up and carried her towards his bed.

in which there are more libraries

Love was too minuscule a word to label what he felt for Rosamund.

She was perfect. Open, welcoming, beautiful, graceful. Everything about her was interesting, from the way she plucked books off the shelf, to the way she smiled at him, to the way she tucked her hair behind her ears. He had come across hundreds of thousands of people across his various lifetimes, and all of them blurred in comparison to her. There was nothing about her that made her particularly special, and yet...

It was everything, all together.

He was entranced. Besotted. Enamored.

He would have to start plucking from other languages in his repertoire to compliment her, because nothing could truly encapsulate Rosamund.

Declan's fingertips ran down her cheek, brushing over her soft skin. She was sleeping once more, something she would do often while so young. Her body was still processing the change, and she was burning through his blood quickly. With her burst of energy, they had fucked once more, first in his bed, and then on the floor beside it.

She had been insatiable and demanding, first sitting on his jaw and then on his cock, and then demanding he fuck her into the floor once more. She had fallen asleep as soon as he finished, and he had scooped her up onto the bed so she could sleep.

A fire was now going in the fireplace to warm the room, something he did not do often, but would resume once more for her. He didn't need the warmth, but he enjoyed the feeling, and he enjoyed the way the fire made the space feel. It was brighter, and warmer in a colorful sense. And the crackling of the wood and the smell of the burning pieces made the entire space feel cozier and intimate.

He wanted everything to be perfect when she woke up. As perfect as she was.

Because they had much to discuss, and so much to do. Like, gathering her belongings so that she could move in with him, and figuring out what to do about her career, and she would need to eat, at some point. That was the most important task of all.

Rosamund moaned as his fingers brushed the side of her neck, and he watched as she opened her eyes, blinking a few times. Her gaze focused on him, and he smiled before leaning down to kiss her. She moaned into the kiss, and he nearly faltered, nearly allowing himself to be sucked back into her, to slide under the covers he was sitting on, so that he could have her again.

He resisted, however, and pulled back to look down at her beautiful face.

"Sleep well?" he asked, and shifted back as she began to sit up.

Rosamund stretched her arms over her head while opening her mouth, only to then close it. It took him a moment to realize what it was—she had planned to yawn, only to not need to. The lack of requirement for oxygen meant that yawning was not something they really needed to do. After a few seconds of stretching, however, he watched her fake a yawn anyways.

Habits, it seemed, would last for some time.

"I slept like the dead," she answered, while stretching a few seconds longer, then dropped her hands into her lap as she laughed. "Well, I guess I am."

Her lips were too full, too perfect, for him to not give into his desire to kiss her. He surged forward, pulling her body to his as he did so, and pressed his lips to hers, silencing her laughter with a kiss. She moaned against him, then climbed into his lap, clearly ready for another round.

It might very well kill him to deny her, and yet, he had to do so.

"You need to feed soon," Declan reminded her as he turned his face away, separating their lips. "This shall have to wait."

"Sex first, and then I feed," she announced, looking rather proud of herself. "I can be patient."

"Mmm, you think you have patience, and yet, the moment you sink your fangs into a human, you will lose yourself entirely."

Rosamund scoffed while running her fingers into his hair. She was distracting, making him lose his sense of priority. He had to get her back on track, and fast.

"After you eat, we can explore the library together," he reminded her.

She stopped in her teasing movements, fingers frozen. She paused, locked up almost, unable to move. He knew it was her vampire senses all trying to keep up with her, and her lack of awareness of time. It would get better, eventually. She would learn to manage.

"Blood, books, then sex," she listed while climbing from his lap. "In that order, and do not try to add something in there."

"You will also need to gather your things so you will have clothes," Declan pointed out, causing Rosamund to roll her eyes.

"I have a change of underwear in the car, but I prefer to be naked around you. Priorities, Declan. We can be naked in the library."

"And when we venture out into the world, exploring other libraries?"

Once again, she froze, but she returned to herself much quicker, a grin spreading over her lips as she rushed towards him. He was nearly knocked over, her supernatural speed surprising him, but he caught her all the same and pulled her close.

Perfect, wonderful, amazing, his little stalkerish archivist who had researched him and tracked him down. Magnificent. Ethereal. Goddess.

His.

"You were serious about exploring more libraries?" she asked, her eyes sparkling a little. "How many?"

Everything. He would give her everything.

"How many are my personal collection? A half dozen or so. How many libraries around the world can we visit? All of them."

He knew he was teasing her, but she seemed to catch his meaning immediately as her eyes widened. "All of them? As in..."

"Rosamund, I'm a couple hundred or thousand or... I'm very old. I have connections. I have loaned a variety of items out to various libraries for their display. Yes, I can gain us access to libraries around the world. The only question is, where do you want to start?"

Her lips quirked into a smile as she tilted her face, mischief clear in her eyes. She was thinking naughty thoughts once more, and he couldn't wait to hear them.

"Change of plans. Sex in the library, and then we eat."

"Rosamund..."

"A quicky, otherwise, I'm going to soak my clean underwear just thinking about the libraries we get to explore."

"And the bookstores," he added.

Her squeal of delight sent blood rushing to his cock. Fuck. She really did need to eat first.

"Have I told you I love you yet?" she asked with a giggle, making his non-beating heart long to stop.

Love... yes, she had, and yet...

"Tell me again when you know it to be true," he murmured as he leaned in against her lips.

"Okay," she whimpered, her lips brushing against his. "Declan, I—"

He kissed her, silencing her words. Love. It was such a small word compared to how he felt, and how he suspected she felt in return. Love was finite, while they were eternal.

And as he whisked them into his library, into the very thing which had seduced her, the gift he would give her a thousand times over...

He loved her with his touch and with his kiss.

And the words to properly explain how he felt, to place the right label on it... they would come with time.

After all, he was her favorite author.

About the Author

Elle M Drew is an avid writer and reader of spicy fantasy and paranormal romance. Her career began with fanfiction and took off from there. Elle infuses a touch of magic into all of her work.

When she isn't busy writing, Elle is exploring Upstate South Carolina with her husband and two kids. She always has iced coffee and a stack of bullet journals on hand for impromptu writing and plotting sessions, and she always has instrumental music playing.

After twenty steamy and extraordinary years of writing fanfiction, she's finally publishing her own books where a magical blend of fantasy and the paranormal mix with dark romance... with an adult, sexy spin, of course.

For more information and news about upcoming releases, visit me online!

Website: ellemdrew.com/

Facebook Group: Off the Rails with Elle M Drew

Tiktok, Instagram, and Threads: @ellemdrewwrites